KARTIKEYA

Anuja Chandramouli is a bestselling Indian author and New Age Indian classicist. Her highly acclaimed debut novel, *Arjuna: Saga of a Pandava Warrior-Prince*, was named by Amazon India as one of the top five books in the Indian-writing category for 2013. *Shakti: The Divine Feminine* (Rupa, 2015), *Kamadeva: The God of Desire* (Rupa, 2014) and *Yama's Lieutenant* are her other bestsellers. Anuja's articles, short stories and book reviews have appeared in various publications like *Femina*, *Women's Era*, *Lonely Planet*, *The Hindu* and *The New Indian Express*. An accomplished orator, Chandramouli regularly conducts storytelling sessions and workshops on creative writing, empowerment and mythology in schools, colleges and on various other platforms. This happily married mother of two little girls lives in Sivakasi, Tamil Nadu, and is a student of classical dance and practitioner of yoga.

Also by the author:

Kamadeva: The God of Desire

Shakti: The Divine Feminine

KARTIKEYA
The Destroyer's Son

ANUJA CHANDRAMOULI

RUPA

Published by
Rupa Publications India Pvt. Ltd 2017
7/16, Ansari Road, Daryaganj
New Delhi 110002

Sales Centres:

Allahabad Bengaluru Chennai
Hyderabad Jaipur Kathmandu
Kolkata Mumbai

ISBN: 978-81-291-4911-4

First impression 2017

10 9 8 7 6 5 4 3 2 1

The moral right of the author has been asserted.

Printed at Thomson Press India Ltd., Faridabad

For the Bickersons.

Contents

Coming to a Boil

THE LOVERS

ℙARVATI HAD NOT dared to believe that such incredible happiness as this could be hers. All she had ever wanted was to belong to Shiva and have him belong to her. It seemed to her that every second of her existence had been spent with his name on her lips, her love for him suffusing every inch of her body and soul. Every moment, every thought, every action was devoted to him alone and nothing else. Aeons had passed with her gazing adoringly at that remarkable face, tranquil yet intense, hoping to memorize every single detail of those unique features while fully submerged in extreme asceticism. Everything she had to offer had been consecrated in his service.

She had been content to be employed thus even as he remained lost to her, consumed by his grief over the passing of his beloved Shakti, oblivious to the fact that she had found her way back to him. He was immersed entirely in the fires of asceticism, allowing its heat to scour him clean of grief and pain, though he would never be entirely free of either.

Kama had tried to bring them together and been destroyed for taking the trouble. She had been devastated on that day. Shiva had looked upon her with love, only to have it replaced with disappointment for she was not his Shakti. Then he had opened his third eye and reduced Kama to a smouldering pile of ashes. His wife Rati had gone berserk with sorrow and Parvati had grieved for both—the deceased Kama and his bereaved spouse, though a part of her was angry with them for meddling. If only they had left them well enough alone!

That was when she had made the happy decision to embark upon the rigorous path Shiva had taken, catch up with him and bring him back. It had been a beautiful journey and she had succeeded beyond her wildest dreams. And now he was hers to hold and love forever. At first, she had been unable to believe it. Haunted by a nameless dread from a past blessed and blighted by love and loss, she had been wary and uncertain.

There was the question of that odious temptress as well, who had shamelessly taken up residence in the thick locks of his hair, thinking to ensnare him with her voluptuous ways and streaming sexuality. This harlot foolishly believed that she had staked her claim to Shiva's heart and clung to him like an invasive shadow but Parvati would not dignify her unwelcome presence in their lives by acknowledging it. Instead she was determined to make the most of the fact that her innermost desire had been granted, focusing on nothing else, not even the unpalatable reality that dreams, even when they came true, would always be sorely lacking in the pure perfection they had promised.

He had thought her shy and bashful. It had taken time, but he had sloughed off the unease that stood as a barrier between them, destroying her fears as he established his eternal mastery over her heart, holding her hand as he threw open the portals of pure pleasure and ushered her inside his life, transporting her to the dizzying realm of endless ecstasy.

Casting away her inhibitions, she surrendered to him and they disappeared into the depths of passion with the shared hope that they need never surface again. They would feast on the delights offered by the other for all time, never tiring of their indulgence in intense love and the shared intimacy that transcended everything. Her happiness was complete.

Parvati would have wished for every one of the creatures in the three worlds to be as joyful as she was and taste the bliss that had become hers. But it was not to be. For too often, unhappiness sprang forth from the sight of another's happiness.

THE DEPOSED MONARCH

Indra, the former King of Heaven, was so full of despair and desperation he was physically sick with it. His eyes were bloodshot, his formerly rock-hard belly distended with drink, and his hair were unkempt, when he arrived to pour out his grievances to Vishnu, the divine Protector.

'Soora's dominion over the three worlds is complete,' he railed at Vishnu, pausing only to quaff his drink, oblivious to the appalled look on Goddess Lakshmi's face which was quickly and courteously masked as she took in the deterioration of a formerly splendid specimen of manhood. He could barely hold his drink owing to the unsteadiness of his hands. Defeat and peevish fury had ravaged his looks as well as his heart and there was something of the cornered beast about him. That probably explained the aura of unsavoury menace that exuded from him like stink from a rotting corpse.

The Goddess took note of these salient details before beating a hasty retreat. What the Devas and her Lord saw in him she would never know. Unmindful of her unease and mild hostility, the object of her ire rambled on.

'His capital city of Mahendrapuri, built on the ashes of Amaravati as well as the blood and bones of the Devas, according to the bloody tale carriers out there, is more marvellous than any before it. Kubera, Yama and Surya are his slaves. My valiant son Jayanta was imprisoned in Soora's dungeons and tortured for days, before he was released on the condition that I hand over every last coin from my treasury if I wanted my son back with all of his body parts intact! Thinking of the horrors they have inflicted on his noble person and childlike psyche has robbed me of my peace of mind and my very sanity!'

'Jayanta will emerge stronger than ever from this experience when Shiva's son arrives to vanquish your foes,' Vishnu consoled him soothingly, although he knew that his loving consort would have recommended horsewhipping some sense into the Lord of Heaven. 'Don't lose heart or hope and place your faith in the deliverer that was promised. You can't see past the dust kicked up by your emotions and it is imperative that you calm yourself. It may not bring you power but it will bring you peace, which is far more precious!'

Indra groaned and belched simultaneously. 'Oh for heaven's sake, have mercy! Don't compound my misery by preaching at me. And while on the subject, when will the Destroyer get around to the business of procreation that will yield us the champion that was promised? My dearest friend, Kama, sacrificed his life to bring Shiva and Parvati together in order to get the divine mother to deliver the promised one who would, in turn, deliver us from evil but his efforts were for nought.

'I had no choice but to sit on my backside and twiddle my thumbs, while Parvati spent aeons propitiating her beloved. Now at long last, the nuptials have been concluded, but after all the drama and death, has the eternally recalcitrant three-eyed God seen fit to oblige us by giving up the fruit of his loins? Of course not!

'Some more aeons have elapsed while they engage endlessly in lovemaking, their everlasting caresses failing to yield the results which we have longed and prayed for over the ages...'

He took a quick breath and a big gulp before resuming his bitter diatribe. 'In the meantime, Soora harasses the mortals and immortals alike with his excesses—torturing our women, enslaving our children, growing fat on his ill-gotten gains, interfering with the Vedic way of life and generally laying waste to the three worlds, having already reduced it to his personal den of pernicious perversions. By the time the boy promised to us, born of Shiva's essence to bring about his long overdue death actually shows up, Soora would have devoured our very existence and shat it out. And all because Shiva is a selfish...'

'Don't!' Vishnu's voice was calm, but Indra sobered up at once, realizing that he had just sprayed the Protector with his spittle as well as the acid of his anger. 'I am sympathetic to the hardships you have endured, but you are viewing things through eyes jaundiced by prejudice and selfish self-interest. Fate has decreed that life will go on, notwithstanding the fluctuations of power, abominations of war and the atrocities of peace.

'Soorapadma is not the best of rulers nor is he the worst, which is why the three worlds have managed to limp by with every indication of normalcy after the Great War ground to a bloody conclusion. The Devas are having the worst of it, for obvious reasons, but the mortals have fared better, wrapped up as they are in the intricacies of a mundane existence and have little more than a passing interest in the divine wielders of power, preoccupied as they are with their own corrupt leaders.

'As a devotee of Shiva, Soora can hardly be accused of interfering with the Vedic way of life, though he has little faith in the Brahmanical rites and rituals so dear to the Devas. Operating outside the bounds of conventional faith does not necessarily make him a villain. Your adversary is hardly the noblest of souls but the same could be said of you as well.'

'How can you say that?' Indra was incensed. 'The Devas don't run around torturing and looting after a victory. There may have been a few unsavoury incidents but that is par for the course after a bit of bloodletting. And the Gods must be propitiated as per the stringent guidelines prescribed by the *Shastras*. Abandoning them is the beginning of the descent into a moral morass that bodes ill for all of us. We cannot just stand by and let it happen! And I have never claimed to be the pinnacle of perfection, but the point is I have always done my best to uphold a certain code of conduct which is more than you can say for the pig who has usurped my position...'

Vishnu interrupted his harangue, 'Shiva and his Shakti have been reunited after too long. Let us not forget the part played by all of us at Daksha's ill-fated *yagna* that led to Shakti's passing. It is to our eternal shame that we allowed those tragic events to transpire. I warned you against the horrendous decision to send Kama to force the Destroyer's hand but you ignored me and the gentle God of Desire perished for it. Listen to me now! Let events run their course. Leave Shiva and his beloved alone.

'They have earned the right to this happy conjoining of body and soul. It is only a matter of time before they turn their attention to the demands of the three worlds and will ensure a surcease to your suffering. Remember, though, that a source of happiness to one is the spring of misery for another and the forces of *purusha* and *prakriti* are constantly at work to redress this imbalance, even as they ferment it. This intense bout of grief you are trapped in will end, and a period of deserved felicity will follow. You will be able to savour it even more, on account of all you have endured.'

Vishnu was not surprised that Indra only stayed long enough to finish his drink, staunchly refusing to derive comfort from his words, choosing instead to flounder in his misery. All he had done was delay the inevitable, for Indra would stay his hand for a while and the newly-weds will have some more borrowed time to themselves. But his impatience would win out and then… What will be, will be. There was no helping these things. Which is why he wasn't even going to try.

THE SOON-TO-BE DEPOSED MONARCH

Soorapadma, the undisputed Lord of the three worlds, had grown heartily sick of it all. He considered himself to be a pragmatic soul and yet, nothing had panned out as he had thought it would. And even when things worked out they did not quite work out because everything left him feeling a little disappointed and vastly deflated.

If inclined to cease and desist with the grousing, Soora

would have admitted that he had little cause for complaint. Along with his brothers Simhamukha and Taraka, he had realized his sainted mother Maya's dream to bring the Devas to their knees and had done so in style. Her father Akhirsen, a powerful Asura King, had been a victim of the infamous duplicity of the Devas and had lost out on the nectar of immortality which he himself had churned from the Ocean of Milk with his own hands. The loss had destroyed the old man and he had extracted a promise from his daughter to seek vengeance. His progenitor, the great Sukracharya had assured the old King that he would keep an eye on Maya and do whatever he could to further the cause of the Asuras.

Maya was as good as her word and had been a hard taskmaster when it came to training her three sons to carry out her will. Soora and his brothers had risen to the occasion magnificently, spending long years in the performance of rigorous penances, before making their bid for power. Now Soora was the undisputed sovereign of the three worlds. For now.

His spies had reported that Shiva had given up his ascetic ways and married Himavan's daughter. Apparently the Devas were jubilant, because their brat would be the slayer of Soora himself. It had made him laugh and his advisors had looked at him as if the news had jarred his brains loose. They had been full of bone-headed ideas, the more ludicrous among which included summoning foul spirits that could penetrate into a womb leaving it barren, or fouler ghouls that feasted on new-born flesh.

Soora had little patience for nonsense so he had given his orders and asked them all to make themselves scarce. The instructions he had issued had been most strict. They were to do nothing. Absolutely nothing. He was Soorapadma, one of the greatest warriors in the history of the three worlds and while he was no saint, he drew the line at spying on the lovemaking of newly-weds and hatching nefarious plots to prevent the conception of their children. That sort of vulgar depravity was exactly the sort of thing his nemesis, Indra, was capable of stooping to, but he would be damned if he was going to cower in fear over an unborn child. Even if the said infant was born to Shiva for the express purpose of killing him.

The way he saw it, the whole thing was, in fact, a tribute to his own formidable prowess as an unmatched conqueror. As a devotee of Shiva himself, it was a telltale sign of the peculiar favour the Destroyer bestowed on his chosen ones, forcing them along dark paths fraught with terror and outright horror, giving them a taste of his raw power which was eerily similar to imbibing poison and feeling its effects. And having put his chosen ones through the wringer, Shiva may choose to bestow on them the gift of *moksha*, although it was equally likely that they be subjected to the perils of his divine will for as long as he deemed it necessary. It was a strangely comforting thought, and it made him feel less depressed.

But he was weary and had been for a long time. Making his mother's dream come true had been about as satisfying as being the ruler of the three worlds, which, as he had confided in Simha and Taraka, was an enormous thorn in the backside. He had done things as a warrior and ruler that, had he been made of anything less than the cast iron of Maya's will, would have seen him teeter off the brink and plunge into the depths of insanity.

Power had given him the biggest high before bringing him lower than a worm's underbelly. It had left a gaping void inside him that no amount of fame, fortune, food, drink and women could fill. And contrary to what his detractors said, he did not force himself on women, though he was insatiable, and the many women—be they mortal or immortal, high-born or low-born, who were more than willing and often fought each other to share his bed had seen no cause for complaint with his unflagging hardihood.

Simha was always counselling him on their duty towards making life better for his subjects and he gave his brother a free hand as well as full access to the treasury to do just that. Many welfare schemes had been implemented to make sure that the unfortunate creatures in his domain had food in their bellies, clothes on their back, decent living conditions and access to medical care.

But he could not help noticing that despite his lionhearted brother's untiring efforts, too many went hungry, naked, lived like pigs in squalor and died too soon, snatched away by some disease or the other. It had been a while since he had bothered to monitor Simha's progress, preferring to drink himself senseless or make reckless love to one of his women when he felt the urge to care even a little about his charges who were doomed to be miserable and live in misery irrespective of what others or they themselves did.

This, of course, meant that not all his subjects worshipped the ground he walked on. The ironical thing was that Simha had about the same number of detractors that he himself had. They had accused him of corruption and violating the virtue of the orphaned children he had taken under his wing. This accusation notwithstanding, he was more popular than Soora, who, in turn, was considered preferable to Taraka whose ceaseless carousing and insatiable appetite for violence made his eldest brother seem saintlike in comparison.

There had been disturbing reports that too many lovers of his, belonging to both sexes, had wound up throttled or tortured to death when his bestial urges and sudden fits of uncontrollable rage were upon him. Possessed of a mercurial disposition, he had originally been as good or bad as the next person. But their mother's death had changed him. Once he had gotten over his depression and found that he had been endowed with an enormous fortune and possessed the power to do exactly as he pleased, Taraka had decided that the greatest of pleasure lay in the abuse of his privileged position.

Henceforth, he went wherever his increasingly perverted instincts led him, barrelling down the serpentine path of unholy vice. Even Simha had once remarked that it would have been vastly preferable if Taraka had contented himself with his whores and indulging his prodigious appetite for food and drink. Instead his passions had grown disturbingly dark.

The elder brothers comforted themselves with the knowledge that Taraka was occasionally known for his sudden displays of generosity or genuine kindness. He was even known to do the right thing by those he had harmed inadvertently, provided he had not killed them outright. But truth be told, they had no idea how to handle their wayward sibling, preoccupied as they were with their own pressing concerns. They were both thankful for Ajamukhi though, their beloved sister. She was an oasis of calm in the middle of all the chaos and she was the only one capable of knocking some sense into Taraka's head.

As for Taraka himself, he loved his elder brothers fiercely and loyally. Ajamukhi had always been his favourite and with their mother gone, she had become his world. Even so, Simha felt, and Soora had to agree, that there was only so much Aja could do. Finally, she had given up on the lot of them. Taraka had taken her departure from their lives badly.

Still, his brothers felt Taraka took things too far when he personally ripped out the tongues of those accused of speaking ill of his siblings, himself or those who exercised particularly bad judgement in referring to the trio as 'sons of a bitch' or dared to cast any other kind of slur on their mother, whom he still worshipped. These he doused in oil and set on fire, after flaying the hide off their backs.

Simha talked to Taraka whenever possible to get him to mend his ways and curb his destructive urges which, if left unchecked, would be the end of him. It did no good, however. Soora had always had a bit of a soft spot for his youngest brother, whom he loved more than his sons. He was even more protective about him given his vulnerability after the passing of their mother and refused to have awkward conversations with him regarding his bedroom antics, though he knew full well that Taraka provided plenty of material for their enemies to use to the brothers' detriment and turn their subjects against them.

And then there was dear Aja. Soora sighed at the thought of his little sister, his lips curling in an affectionate smile. Without doubt, she was the best of them all and the only one worthy to wield power, if only because of how resistant she had always been to its lure. If his mother had not been so resentful of her prodigious charm and extraordinary talents, things would have gone differently for her. And Aja would have been blessed with the happiness that she deserved. It pained him to think of his little sister and he rubbed his temples, hoping for blessed relief.

The long and short of it was that Soora had grown weary,

Simha had turned philosophical, and Taraka had become whatever it was that he had become. The good news was that an end was in sight. For better or for worse.

His thoughts turned to the unborn son of Shiva and Parvati. The only one who would have the endless reservoirs of raw power needed to destroy the mighty sons of Sage Kashyap and Maya. It confounded him, but the very thought thrilled his embattled spirit and filled his heart with a strange ecstasy. Perhaps he *was* losing his mind, as his advisors suspected.

GANGA

It was not the first time Shiva's audacity had galled her and it wouldn't be the last, but it did not stop her from becoming so furious with him she could barely restrain herself from resisting the urge to bear down on him with all the might of her elemental power and crush him with the tremendous force of her reckless, entirely uninhibited descent. The way she had attempted to do so when the mortal Bhagiratha had beseeched her to come down from heaven and bless his uncles, the fallen sons of Sagara, with salvation.

Legend had it that the Gods had begged Shiva to contain the unstoppable Ganga in his locks to prevent her from washing away all life. But she alone knew otherwise. It had been at her own sly insinuation that Bhagiratha had been inveighed into delivering the Destroyer to her. And unlike her rival, she did not have to engage in supremely uncomfortable and inconvenient penances to win her Lord!

What a fight she had put up though when her chosen lover had unloosed his magnificent locks to contain her in the wild tangles and matted locks so deliciously unique to him! How she had struggled! And his response had been to tighten his grip on her wild spirit which would never be tamed without her express consent. It tickled her pink to think that the foolish mortals revered his ability to have succeeded in imprisoning her. As if such a thing would ever be possible! How could they not know that her gushing, surging waters could quench the flaming power of the Destroyer in a heartbeat? Therein lay her strength, for unlike him, she knew better than to use her powers to destroy.

And so they danced to the music she had composed and which only he could hear, for all of eternity. She struggled and struggled and he embraced her harder and harder, determined to never ever let her go. It was what she had wanted all along. All that effort he expended towards keeping her as a part of him meant that he loved her as much or even more than she did. It had to be true. And it made her so giddy and exuberant, she would have willingly died in the suffocating crush of his masculine energy, which she craved like a drug.

And thus they had remained in this state of mutual intoxication, with only Ganga being wise to the masterful snare she had entrapped him in, letting him think that he had mastered her. And then he had gone and married that Parvati while still being unable to let go of her. He was addicted to the feel of Ganga's silken caresses as they wantonly trickled over his body, released in tiny streams from the wilderness of the jungle that was his hair and revelled in her touch even as the heat of his passion fuelled the lovemaking he was engaged in with his insipid and boring new bride, who made love with the awkwardness of a perennial virgin.

Once again, she marvelled at the sheer audacity of the male of the species. And to think that when she had her little flirtatious dalliance with Vishnu who had a foot fetish, he had put paid to any other erotic adventure she may have chosen to have by making a willing captive out of her. But of course, she was expected to be a mute witness to his endless canoodling.

But truth be told, this tickled her pink as well. She could feel Parvati's jealousy and it gave her a perverse sense of satisfaction. For it was acknowledgement of the fact that it was Ganga alone of all who had loved him to death, who got to be an actual physical part of him. Whereas in her rival's case, the moment Shiva withdrew, as he eventually would have to, she would have no choice but to resign herself to his loss.

Of course, Parvati being possessed of the conniving tricks so characteristic of their sex, despite her austere holy consort act, would no doubt seek to bind her to him, by popping out a little brat to quickly lay claim to the exalted station of being the mother of Shiva's son. But that was yet to happen, and it may never come to that, if Ganga had anything to do with it. It was about time Shiva realized that not even he could get away with everything.

ANANGA

He was Ananga, the 'bodiless one'. It was a pity really, because back in his heyday, he had been the handsomest of them all, with the kind of sculpted physique that made women swoon and the men sick with envy. But that was all before he had incurred the wrath of the Destroyer and been reduced to dust and then, nothing.

It was a long story which had happened a long time ago and too much had already been written about it. He was usually portrayed as a meddling pimp or a charming fool but you got over that sort of injustice when a few aeons had elapsed and every one of the thousand things you had cared so damned much about were reduced to the trifling inanities they had been to start with. So mostly he was not as upset as he had once been. Mostly.

Desire had been the domain over which he ruled and still did. The messiest, yet most sublime of feelings, it had come into being when life sought in vain to defy death. On the best of days, it had been a notoriously difficult job and meting the damn thing out in just the right proportions had proved nigh impossible. Too many had been consumed by the passion it provoked and even more had been condemned to a sterile existence leached of its delicious flavour.

His job had not become easier but the good news was that he could no longer be devoured by its demands simply because there was nothing left of him to swallow whole and spit out. The Destroyer had done a thorough job and all that remained was his essence scattered pell-mell among the tools of his trade—the mango and lotus blossoms, honey and wine, birds and bees, roses and thorns, silvery moonlight and loving hearts.

Memories lingered and he would have liked to have let them go and would have, if they had not been so precious. Because they kept his love alive and close to him though cruel fate, time and distance had conspired to keep them apart. He watched over her across the unbridgeable chasm that separated them, wishing he could do more to comfort her as she grieved endlessly over his loss even after the debilitating pain had been reduced to a dull ache.

Her love was such that she alone could see him. Although she would never be able to hold him, run her fingers through his hair or hit him with lotus stalks the way she had in the days of yore. The unbearable tragedy was that in her eyes, he had been diminished to something that was even less than the ghost of his former self. But it was all they had besides their dreams, so they made do with it. They had to.

In the landscape of shared dreams, they sometimes made love with feverish haste knowing they would always be interrupted by rude awakening sooner rather than later. Both liked to hold hands or disappear into a loving embrace. Mostly they conversed endlessly pouring out their need for each other through the insufficient medium of words.

'Shiva and Parvati are together now,' she told him what everybody knew. 'I should be happy for them but instead I am consumed with envy. It is unworthy of me, but I would rather they were both dead. Their happiness is more than I can bear, especially after the fact that our love was the price paid to bring them together. I cannot stand it!'

'Your unhappiness tears at my heart!' He breathed in the intoxicating scent of her luxuriant hair, which had all the potency of a retrieved memory. 'Shiva paid heed to your penances and promised that we would be reunited, remember? It is only a matter of time before we are restored to each other.'

'He had no right to take you away from me! It was unspeakably wicked of him, especially since you were only trying to give him the gift of the greatest desire of his heart and reunite him with the love of his life. What we have lost will never be returned in its original state. And oblivious to our loss, he makes love to his wife so passionately, lost to the rest of the three worlds. I hope something terrible happens to them! It is evil of me, but I genuinely want Parvati to know what it feels like to lose something dear to her!'

'Hush! Something terrible did happen to Shiva. He knew

loss too and at the height of his suffering, pain was all he had to
mete out. But now that he has rediscovered happiness, nothing
but good will come of it. Wishing harm on others will rebound
on us and even if tragedy strikes them, you will derive no
happiness from it, so what is the point of ill will?

'I know it is hard but let go of your anger and remember
that our love will survive anything, even the wrath of the
Destroyer! You need to stop being so afraid. Have faith in us,
if nothing else. Things may never be the same between us but
nevertheless what we have will always be special.'

'You are right!' Rati said, immediately contrite, and his
phantom heart contracted with the love he bore her. 'I am the
unworthy one, no different from the meanest of the mortals
and immortals who have cast the evil eye on Shiva and his
beloved. While they are joined thus, they complete each other
and have no need of anyone or anything else. I fear that the
combined envy of the less fortunate will bring harm upon
them. If anything untoward were to happen to them now, I will
not be able to bear it!'

'There is no need for guilt. Fate spares none and Shiva
is bound by the consequences of his actions the same way
everyone else is. But even if misfortune awaits them, borne by
the strength of your righteous resentment, it will not do lasting
damage but become transformed as ever by the power of the
good that still remains in all of us, and something beautiful will
emerge from their tragedy, as a monument to abiding love.

'It will be a wondrous gift that will keep on giving and
forever be a divine blessing to the denizens of the three worlds.
Mark my words, the bounty of true love is always precious but
this one will be doubly so and will be cherished forever by all of
us!'

Miraculous Origin

$\mathscr{P}$ATIENCE HAD NEVER been Indra's strong suit; neither was an ability to see past his immediate needs. All he wanted was the complete annihilation of Soora and his brothers, so that all that was rightfully his would be restored to him. Ideally, he would have preferred all of this to come to pass a few centuries ago and he could no longer wait for Shiva and Parvati to get on with it.

Which was why he summoned the ragtag bunch of Devas who were in hiding with him and not currently employed in waiting on Soora at his pleasure, stubbornly insisting that they pay a visit to the newly-weds and beg their favour. Needless to say, they were all squeamish with Agni and Vayu being particularly vociferous in their protest that his royal command was not in keeping with decorum or even common decency. Naturally, Indra had decreed that the task of actually approaching the divine couple with their request would fall to the dissenting pair.

None of them had forgotten what had happened to the last Deva who had dared to disturb the Destroyer although he had protested till he was blue in the face and Indra had issued a royal command, practically forcing him into the foolhardy act that had been the death of him. Mute horror was registered on the faces of Vayu and Agni. Both could not help thinking that they would have been better off in Soora's dungeons being subjected to the tender mercies of his dreaded torturers, or taken into his employ and given the task of emptying chamber pots.

Indra tried in vain not to notice their terror, but he felt a pang at the memory of his dear departed friend. Unable to still his conscience, he amended his decision and said they would all go together to add their voices to Vayu and Agni's. 'You are Lord of the Flames, and fire cannot destroy fire,' he told Agni bracingly, adding to Vayu for good measure, 'and even Shiva's fire can be put out by the mighty Lord of the Winds!' He realized that he was lying through his teeth but there was no help for it. It was time for Shiva's son to be born, whether his parents liked it or not.

In due course, they found themselves on the upper reaches of Mount Kailasha, arguing with the Ganas who denied them entrance with more than their usual belligerence. 'The Lord and his consort are not to be disturbed!' they were informed firmly. They brandished evil-looking weapons menacingly and their eyes were brimming with so much contempt, it left the petitioners in little doubt as to their thoughts on folks who sought to barge in on a pair of newly-weds.

Vayu and Agni had begun to slink away when Indra stopped them in their tracks with his most repressive glare. Raising his voice in what he hoped was devotional fervour and not an impatient summon, he began singing songs in praise of Shiva, signalling that the others join him. And they did so, reluctant and tremulous at first. Their voices growing in strength as they resigned themselves to the course of action they had been coerced into taking up. It was about time they were delivered from evil too, so why not?

Later they were punished for their intemperate behaviour but in all fairness, they were not entirely responsible. For the time had come. After waiting for aeons and aeons, it all seemed to materialize in a single heartbeat. There was a sudden unforeseen shifting that sent ripples across the three worlds as bits of fiery stars, glowing embers and cosmic dust realigned themselves letting off dazzling sparks, pulsating slowly at first and growing stronger as the intensity built with the sudden surge in the currents of universal energy.

Mangala, the planet Mars, had ascended and six of the seven stars in the heavenly constellation known as the Pleiades, the *Kartika nakshatra*, shone bright in anticipation of a most propitious event, even as the other constellations grew paler and throbbed with feverish anticipation. The air currents swirled as the fiery planet unleashed its unbridled energy and all living things experienced a stirring in their blood. Uncontrollable excitement and nervous anticipation escalated to unbearable heights as their hearts pounded in keeping with the cosmic rhythms that had become increasingly frenzied.

It was a time of heightened potency, heralding an event that would change the course of history, the ramifications of which would reach far into the future to the very end of time. The three worlds had been buffeted by war, strife and endless turmoil. The living had lost their faith, hopelessly corrupted by the allure of materialistic gain. Famine and plague had ravaged the land and further besieged dying spirits. Mother Earth shuddered with the intensity of it, as events coalesced, leading to one incandescent moment in time.

The voices of the Devas rose higher and higher, vibrations from their primeval need, reverberating across the three worlds, as the chanting rose to a steady crescendo, the sound of 'OM' exploding from their hearts, its timeless beat throbbing with raw power. Hypnotized, the Ganas added their voices to those of the Devas, as did the *rishis*, animals and birds.

Vayu and Agni, propelled forward by the hand of destiny, seized the moment to draw closer to the mouth of the cave, keeping their eyes averted from the couple within. With a sudden cry, Parvati pulled herself free, wrenching apart from her lover, experiencing a feeling of loss so profound, the tears spilled freely from her eyes, blinding her as she retreated into the dark interiors of the caves. The sound of mocking laughter rang out in her ears and she fled from it.

At the same moment, Shiva spilled his seed, calm and resigned to what must be. The silvery fluid flew through space in a steady arc, burning every single one of the Devas with its unbearable heat and they sank to their knees, their bellies engorged with the essence of the Destroyer as it sucked the life out of them. Every minute cell was in acute agony and they screamed in anguish.

Agni had acted on reflex, gathering the seed in his palms and fleeing thoughtlessly as it scorched him, burning every single atom that constituted his being. At that moment, he experienced first-hand, the agony of being burnt alive, living the fate of countless victims claimed by the fire he commanded. Thanks to his heightened consciousness, he actually felt his flesh burn and his blood boil, exploding out of his tortured body in a burst of scalding steam.

Vayu tried to stay as close to him as possible, withstanding the heat marginally better than his fellow celestial but knowing that it was too much for any of them to bear. It was the Destroyer's limitless power contained in his seed. The winds he commanded would never be up to the task of putting out those flames. And yet, he summoned the coolest breezes only to have the moisture sucked out of them within moments.

The duo disappeared into the distant skies, Agni holding Shiva's seed in his cupped palms, and taking it in his mouth when it burnt through his hands. Buffeted endlessly by unbearable pain, but determined to bear it for as long as he could, because he must, he went on and on and on. Vayu tried to keep up, terrified of the burden he would have to shoulder but fully resolved to see it through to the end.

Parvati clutched her womb, and her cry was that of a wounded animal. Brushing aside the loving arms that encircled her shoulders offering a measure of comfort, she stormed to the entrance of the cave, standing tall in naked splendour, eyes flashing and her dishevelled hair whipping about, scourging her body, slick with perspiration. The Devas cowered at her feet. Even if they had not been doubled over in excruciating torment, not one of them would have mustered the courage to meet her gaze.

'You have taken something that was mine by right,' she began, her voice a whiplash that easily flayed the skin off their cringing backs, leaving only bloodied pulp behind, 'blinded as ever by your unceasing selfishness and endless pettiness. Mark my words, my child will be restored to me, for I am blameless. As for your wives, their wombs will remain arid and barren forever. The three worlds have suffered enough from your trespasses and will no longer be forced to endure the ordure from your unworthy loins!

'Go now, before I lose control of myself and crush the life out of every single one of you, leaving the remains for the carrion creatures to feed on, which is more than you stinking parasites deserve. None of you are worthy enough to bear the essence of my Lord, and it will vacate your bodies after scouring it clean!'

Her chest heaved with the vehemence of her grief and rage as the Devas fled pell-mell in terror, scurrying like rats from her presence. The Ganas prostrated themselves at her feet, cursing themselves for failing to keep intruders at bay, weeping in dismay, and begging for forgiveness as she stalked away without a backward glance.

This time, she fled into the embrace of her beloved, weeping into his chest, imbibing his calm aura, allowing it to flood through her distraught senses, wondering even as she did so, how it was that he could be so unaffected by the calamity that had overtaken them.

'These creatures deserved to be incinerated by your third eye so much more than poor Kama whose intentions at least were noble and yet you spare them! Not only that, you seem so at peace with what had just happened! As for me, I am so distressed, I can't stand it!' she sobbed into his chest.

He replied in measured tones, gently heading off her anger, 'They have been waiting a long time for a son to be born to us and simply ran out of patience. I have never been as invested in their affairs as they would like me to be, and it has always been their wish to avail themselves of my power without the rigorous effort that needs to be expended if I am to oblige. Even then, as you know, mostly it turns out to be more than they bargained for.

'My seed had been charged by the power of penance, and if I had discharged it into your womb, its power would have been neutralized which would not really suit the purpose of those who have need of the Destroyer's son to vanquish their enemies now, would it?'

'The power of your seed will certainly not be quenched in the life-giving waters of my womb!' she flared at him, though the worst of her rage had subsided. 'It would have been tempered and strengthened with our son inheriting the best of both of us! Those self-serving louts merely want a warrior, brought forth from your loins, armed with nothing but a capacity for destruction and a killing frenzy who will inflict death mindlessly on their command. It will never come to pass, mark my words... Not if I have anything to do with it!'

'You don't seem to have a very high opinion of my powers...' Shiva pretended to be offended.

'You know I am your greatest devotee,' she responded in all seriousness, 'but that does not alter the fact that without me, you are nothing. If I were not around to take care of you and clean up after your excesses, the unholy mess would create a terrible stink!'

Parvati was silent for several long moments and Shiva waited patiently, content to hold her in his arms. 'He is mine,' she murmured softly, it was not a question. 'My own son! Nobody can succeed in taking him away from me, any more than those who would seek to separate us. I will find him and raise my boy with these very hands. And he will be the best of them all, greater even than his father because he will always be his mother's son!'

Journey Through the Elements

AGNI HAD DONE his best but he could not bear the power of Shiva's seed a moment longer. The contents of his mouth spilled out in a rush, to be snatched up by Vayu, leaving him behind, drained and dangerously close to the ashes his own devouring flames usually left behind. The Wind God howled, as his own odyssey of suffering and salvation began.

In that moment, Agni's fiery gaze, sanctified and intensified by the Destroyer's potency, successfully pierced the heavy veils of time. He saw himself severely censored and derided for his actions in carrying Shiva's seed in his palms and mouth. There was punishment in store for him as well. It did not bother him in the least. He had lived through a trial by fire, and he did not find himself wanting. That was all that mattered. It did not behove him to bother in the least about the mean-spiritedness of those who spent their lives wrinkling up their noses at others, in protest of the foul odours that they did not seem to realize emanated from their own malodorous selves.

Silently, he wished Vayu luck. Like Agni, he too was blessed and a chosen one of Shiva. They were truly amongst those favoured greatly by fortune.

At that moment in time, Vayu was feeling as far from fortunate as it was possible to feel, faring even worse that the Lord of Fire had. The winds he commanded bore him up and away, but there was no escaping the unendurable torment. He could feel an inferno build at the very core of his being and it threatened to erupt out of him. His eyeballs bulged, expanding inexorably, as the heat intensified, threatening to burst in a grisly explosion of superheated jelly.

In those burning moments, Vayu died a thousand deaths, yet he had never been more fiercely alive. Through his feverish, bloodshot eyes and the swirling currents of the gale winds his besieged person had conjured up, Vayu espied Ganga, a vision in silver, decked out in diaphanous garments that showed off her voluptuous assets to their best advantage. He stared at the curves of her body, forgetting even his extreme torment on the altar of her beauty.

She was sitting pretty at the very summit of the Himalayas, with the snowflakes swirling around her and adorning those magnificent, unloosed tresses in a shower of pearls. Enormous eyes twinkled at him, inviting and mischievous. Clearly the Goddess was deriving enormous amusement from his sorry plight.

Her waters cascaded down the slopes of the mountain range in a silvery rush and slowed to a gentler roil as they wound their way through the jewelled valleys of Mother Earth amidst a plenitude of blooms and a shimmering carpet of emerald green. Vayu needed no further prompting and summoning a final burst of wind, despite his depleted strength, he deposited the holy seed into the outstretched arms of Ganga.

She gathered it to her bosom, welcoming the searing heat and pain, embracing the very essence of the one she loved, revelling in the gloriously intimate feel of it. Her waters simmered and came to a boil, killing the living creatures that had made the depths and swirling currents their home, bearing testament to the unstoppable strength and savagery of Shiva's seed. Meting out death to every one of Ganga's children, it came to life spurred into being by their passing.

Pain exploded in Ganga, and her currents gorged themselves on it as she held on for all she was worth, laughter bubbling over from her lips, even as the temperature of her body rose to unendurable levels turning her into a molten river of fire. 'This is Shiva's son alright!' she trilled, with a blackened tongue, unmindful of the fact that her hair had been singed off and her perfect beauty was now charred beyond recognition. 'Every bit as masterful and intractable as his father. And as his mother, I bestow upon him the indomitable will and unstoppable force of the Goddess Ganga. May he always prevail over his enemies and win the hearts of all he seeks to conquer!'

She had not known that her heart could burgeon with so much love for this special child and be filled to overflowing. Boiling hot tears spilled down her cheeks, inflicting severe damage on the ruins of her face and chest. Ganga barely noticed, and even if she had, she could not have cared less, lost in the agony and ecstasy of the moment as well as the whirlwind of her thoughts.

Parvati could never understand Shiva the way Ganga did. There she was moaning and groaning, whining about having lost the chance to carry Shiva's seed in her womb, having hoped, no doubt, that her belly would grow fat on his distillate and dreamed about delivering his child while he held her hand like a dutiful husband and householder. Hah! As if things would ever be that simple with the three-eyed God! As if he or his son would ever be bound by the ridiculous diktats of convention and rely on cumbersome vessels to fulfil their plans!

Ganga would have liked to hold on forever but the time had come for the child to be born on Earth. Digging deep for every ounce of strength she could dredge up, not to hold on but to let go, Ganga with a final outpouring of affection, deposited Shiva's seed which was already beginning to take shape, on her banks, amongst the verdant greenery of Saravana, the forest of reeds.

It burst into flames instantly, conflagrating everything in sight, throwing up thick clouds of acrid smoke that choked the life out of all in the vicinity. Ganga watched for a long time as the fire raged on and on, through the hot tears that blinded her. Bruised and burnt, inside as well as out, she felt drained, yet rejuvenated. She had not experienced anything this powerful since her torrid tussle with the Destroyer. But her work was done and it was time to bid her farewell to the child she had claimed a part in bringing to being.

Still crying, though even Ganga did not know whether they were tears of joy or sorrow, she withdrew to Shiva. And captivity. For the first time, she empathized with her rival. Now she too knew what it was like to have something one cared for more deeply than anything else cruelly wrenched away from her.

Behind her, Saravana burned. Walls of fire and smoke danced every which way, devouring life wherever their reach extended on heaven and earth. Birds and beasts, men and women, young and old—were consumed to sate a ravenous appetite which showed no sign of letting up, though it eventually did.

Once the fire died down, with the suddenness with which it had begun, there was a stillness in the air, and all things in creation held their collective breaths, releasing it only when the pregnant pause was broken by the age-old cry of newborn children. And there, amidst the glowing embers, lay six baby boys of such surpassing beauty, they stole the breath away. Lustily they wailed for their mothers, impatient to be held and fed.

The incessant cries were raucously melodious and alluring as a siren's call. And as it turned out, the imperious summons were in turn rapturous and deadly for those who responded. Those who paid heed to the call would never know a moment's regret for having done so without sparing a thought for the consequences. Because he would always be worth it.

A Cluster of Lustrous Mothers

THERE WERE HUNDREDS of them, an amalgam of heat and energy, clustered together in the night sky. The dimmest of them shone brighter than a million suns. The brightest and most luminous of them all, were six sisters—the Kartikas, who ruled over the rest. They were guardians of the perennial light, the flameless fires of multiple hues that was the source of all life and must never be extinguished. It was their job to keep it burning bright at all times, and so they kept vigil, forever alert to danger or threats, both internal and external on the endless watch that must extend to cover all of eternity.

The Kartikas were cognizant of the six sparks, long before they emerged from the roiling, ever-changing pillar of light they had sworn to serve. A gift from the Godhead born of need and willed by the fates. It was the rarest of occurrences that happened less than a handful of times over the incalculable *kalpas*. The inexorable wheel of time would come full circle many more times, before such a wondrous event would take place again.

The sparks were a rare coming together of fragments, bits and pieces from the very wellspring of the Destroyer's potent and often dangerous quiddity. Once it coalesced, an invincible weapon of boundless power would come into being, capable of saving and annihilating the universe, depending on what it was called to do. Irrespective of the course of action it would choose to pursue, history would be inalterably changed by the emergence.

They knew what needed to be done. Their services were needed to protect the child that would emerge from the sparks. To them fell the honour of caring for this infant, till he was ready to do what he was born to do, keeping him safe from the fell forces that would seek to claim and subvert him for their own dark purposes. There was little time to be wasted.

And so it was that the Kartikas took birth as the wives of great seers, who had devoted their lives to the mastery of asceticism. The guardians of the light spent their days in peace and quiet, almost completely given over to the humdrum chores of a monotonous existence with the home and hearth claiming most of their attention. And yet, the tiniest and the best part of them never lost sight of the purpose, for which they had been born. It waited and watched, with a patience so exquisite that it lit them up from within.

Unobtrusively, they monitored the heavens day after day, ever vigilant, alert for the time when the child would have need of them. They sensed his coming long before the Destroyer nudged him into being, sensitive to his ephemeral effluvium, which the all-pervasive ether wafted over to them. Buoyant with expectant exhilaration, their spirits took flight in heady anticipation making them feel strong and special, more loved than their noble husbands had ever made them feel.

The bawling of the infants from far away came to them with a crash and roar, splendid in the dreadful ruckus raised. It was music to their ears and from the very first moment they heard that mellifluous cry that resonated with the cadences of the primordial 'Om' which harkened back to the very beginning of time, they were lost to themselves. Forever more, all that would matter would be their great love for the child who had been given unto their care, no doubt in recognition for every meritorious deed they had had the good sense to perform over the course of the endless cycle of birth and rebirth.

In unison, they raced in the direction of the incessant wailing that tugged at their heartstrings and made their eyes tear. So anxious were they and desperate in their all-consuming need to reach the little ones, whose cries, majestic as the roaring of a lion, drew them so powerfully, the Kartikas were unmindful of the thorns they tread on and wayward branches that tore at their garments and hair, putting them in a state of immodest dishabille.

Breathless and dishevelled, they found themselves on the banks of the river Ganga. There, nestled among the reeds which had tightened around them in a protective embrace, lay six baby boys, cheeks ruddy from their lusty bawling which had grown to such a furious pitch the eardrums threatened to shatter.

For a moment, they stood still as they took in the sight of their divine charges, their hearts fit to bursting with love they had not known they were capable of feeling. Falling over each other in their haste, they gathered a screaming baby in each of their arms, tearing off the remains of their upper garments to offer nipples engorged with milk for the infants to suckle upon.

In the ensuing silence, broken only by the contented sounds of suckling and cooing, the Kartikas knew that perfect happiness was theirs at last. The bonds of the flesh and spiteful civilization were loosened, making way for pure sensation to inundate their being, causing the spirit to exult with the sheer joy and beauty of it. In a heightened state of awareness, everything was felt more keenly and supping on the raw exultance of motherhood, they felt themselves, finally and utterly complete.

And thus, they remained lost to all else but the needs of the child in their care, attending to his every need, forgetting the world around them in the process. Time and place no longer had any meaning and the Kartikas were conscious only of the wee babies in their care, wrapped up in a state of total bliss.

Each used her own discarded garments to swaddle the little one assigned to her protection, and rocked him in her lap. They sang together, loud and joyously making the little ones babble merrily as they listened to their mothers, imbibing the love they poured into the words. Sometimes the tunes were silly, full of nonsensical rhymes made for inducing laughter. At other times, it was profound, filled with the lessons and wisdom they had gleaned over the ages.

Snugly ensconced in the pillowy softness of their mothers' laps, each one listened with perfectly formed eyebrows, crinkled up with a hoary philosopher's gravity, to tales of great deeds performed throughout the course of history which they assured him he was sure to surpass. They sang of great wars fought to make sure that the light never went out, keeping the darkness that would otherwise engulf them all forever at bay. They sang of gods and demons, men and women, saints and sinners, all of whom would come under his protection.

The days passed in a furious blur as the children grew up with rude haste and in robust health, thriving on the endless attention and affection that was lavished on them. Their mothers were so wrapped up in their charges, they had forgotten entirely about their revered spouses, who had worked themselves into a fine lather when the news reached them that their wives had delivered bouncing babies. They received the happy tidings with ill-concealed fury, since not one of them had performed their husbandly duties with their lovely wives for many years now.

By dint of the tremendous powers they wielded on account of their ascetic merit, the husbands, who were mortified by the cuckold's horns their wives had forced them to wear, returned to their forest homes in great haste to be confronted by the sight of their wives, looking plump and radiant, bedecked in scanty apparel that hid nothing, engaged in active pursuit of a gaggle of infants who were tearing about on chubby legs and raising all manner of hell. The sound of raucous laughter was the fuel poured in liberal quantities over the already raging flames of their wrath. Already the good denizens of the forest had gathered at their back, delighted at the prospect of a scurrilous scandal.

'Filthy whores!' their enraged voices rang out in unison, 'How dare you flaunt your infidelity in our faces? Was it too much to hope that you stayed pure while we engaged in penances for the betterment of the three worlds? You are no better than bitches in heat, fit only for...'

The sages would have liked to vent their spleen longer, but the diatribe was cut short when the precocious infants pelted them with stones, sensing that their beloved mothers were the recipients of the attack and refusing to stand for it. They hurled sticks, stones and all the mud that could be gathered in their baby fists, ignoring the half-hearted admonishments of their mothers who were trying and not succeeding in stifling their mirth at the sight of their dignified husbands whose snowy white robes had been bespattered with mud and flowing tresses festooned with bits of twigs or forest foliage.

It was the final straw that broke their backs and the sages were frothing at the mouths much to the delight of the mob that had gathered behind them, anxious to show their support and take the sisters down a peg or two for being so confoundedly different. Besides how could they stay away when there were half-naked women to be ogled at and censured? If they were lucky, a curse or two would be roundly pronounced and blood would flow in earnest...

There were women in that angry mob as well, baying for the blood of their rivals who dared to be so uninhibited and worse, so unabashedly happy! Motherhood had not made them glow with such vulgar happiness, instead it had devoured their looks and youth both, leaving them leached of their vitality. They too would have liked to have had torrid affairs and enjoy the pleasures of illicit sex like those wanton women but no, fate had decreed nothing quite as exciting for them. It was unfair and someone had to pay!

'Admit your guilt!' the sages called out, feeding on the hostility of those around them, 'And we will give your bastards the mercy of a quick death by drowning every one of the products of your infidelity in the holy waters of Ganga! You will pay the price for your unbridled lust by having your heads tonsured and your polluted bodies pelted with stones. If Yama is kind, he will take you to his thousand hells where the Yamaduttas will make you answer for your sins with the tools of their trade and you can spend eternity regretting your sinful indulgence of base passion!'

'They must be burnt alive! Their dying cries will serve as a warning to those who stray!' voices rang out on all sides.

By way of reply, the Kartikas quietly picked up their children, strapping them to their backs and stood erect, proud and regal in their bearing, calm and dignified. Not a single soul bothered to refute the slanderous claims that were being levelled at them. Their eyes alone flashed a warning...but the sages would not pay heed.

Bolstered by the vociferous support, the sages chanted incantations, their strident voices filled with malice and deadly intent which summoned wild beasts of prey and foul ghouls to tear apart their adulterous wives and feast on the flesh of the fruit of their befouled wombs. The crowd shouted their approbation, hissing and spitting at the Kartikas who continued to display godless temerity in banding together, ready to battle it out without a hint of embarrassment.

Summoning up the sheer savagery and deadliness which only a mother protecting her young can, they fell upon the forces of darkness unleashed upon them, rending and tearing as they destroyed those who would dare to harm their own. The thwarted hordes fell upon the mob and all around there were the sounds of cracked bones, heavy blows, flesh tearing, a symphony of senseless slaughter—as the Kartikas threw back wave upon wave of the fell minions conjured by the vituperative vehemence of their foolish husbands.

Showers of blood bathed them and their charges who did not cry at the sight of the carnage but displayed every sign of enjoyment as blood spattered and pooled around them, in the middle of the mad carnage. Realizing that they were battling forces beneath their yen, the sages ceased their incessant chanting, spearing their wives with venomous looks of intense loathing.

'Godless animals!' they cried, taking in their bloodstained garments, heaving breasts and teeth bared in uniform snarls, still in a killing frenzy. All around was the telltale evidence of carnage as the furry bodies lay separate from limbs and spines that had been torn out. A black cloud mushroomed to the heavens, carrying with it the stink of incinerated ghouls who had been consumed by the fury of the Kartikas.

'Fall at our feet and pray for forgiveness! Spend the rest of your lives in prayer and penance! Cast aside the children of your sin or the three worlds will know of your infamy and will spit on you for being whores! You will forever be known as the loose women whose husbands cast them aside unable to look upon those whose bodies have been soiled by foul desire and souls stained by sin! No man will ever have you, now and forever more!'

'Blind fools!' the Kartikas spat out, 'We spare your lives not out of compassion but because you are unworthy to die at our hands! How dare you talk of virtue after setting upon defenceless babies in this despicable manner? Return to the false rites and rituals you value over kindness and good sense. Live on, knowing that you have just lost something indescribably precious which will never be restored to you. Know that our hearts and souls, minds and bodies will always belong to the one who is truly worthy of it!'

'Hah!' the sages retorted, 'Having used you up, the blackguards who tempted you into straying will discard you like the pieces of filth you are. Doomed to wander the three worlds with only your accursed sisters for company, robbed of lover and lawful Lord, you will know pain, the likes of which cannot be endured and then you may regret at leisure, praying in vain for the death you cheated on this day!' And with that last barb, uttered with every last ounce of their inexhaustible hatred, they were gone.

Drained and enervated, the Kartikas huddled together drawing warmth and comfort from the tiny little bodies that were pressed close to them. They held on tightly, wishing that they could stay this way forever but already preparing themselves to let their love go. For the perfect little world that had been theirs to inhabit so short a while ago had been shattered and piecing it together would be an exercise in futility.

Still, they were happy to have had their brief tryst with unalloyed joy when sparks from an empyrean realm had rained down upon them and drawn them into the very heart of the light. It was enough. And always would be.

Mother and Son

$\mathcal{T}$HE GANAS FOUND them like that, the Kartikas and the six little bodies, entwined so closely together, they looked like an extended conurbation of tangled limbs, hair and warm flesh. It was a strangely poignant sight and they stood still for a moment, just breathing in the scent of heady love, before reporting back to Parvati as they had been told to do.

Battle-hardened veterans, they nevertheless cried openly with naked joy. Shiva's son, the child who would hold the hands of all who lived in the three worlds and lead them to redemption, was here at last. He was the answer to their prayers, a fulfilment of a long-standing and deeply cherished dream. They were glad and made haste. It was time to reunite mother and son.

Initially it had been difficult for Parvati to deal with the whole thing. She resented having her son snatched away from her womb and arms. Agni, Vayu and Ganga had played her false. But that was to be expected, especially from the treacherous nest of vipers the Devas had become and the wily vixen who had manipulated her way into Shiva's matted locks, if not his heart. Hardest to bear was her dear husband's attitude in all of this.

While it may have seemed that the uncouth intervention of the Devas had caused him to spill his seed, she knew him well enough to know that its tumultuous voyage had his design writ all over it. Loving him was an endless saga of tumult and tempestuous passion. Not that his romance with her was going to be all smooth sailing, she had mused with a small grimace. If Shiva thought his will would prevail in this matter, he would do well to think again. Without the power of Shakti that had been revived in her, not a single one of them, or anything at all in creation would amount to much.

'The time will come when my son will need me. Only me,' she mused to herself, 'and I will be ready to do everything in my power not only to help him but to temper my Lord's concentrated power roiling inside him with the distillate of my own essence.' In the meantime, there was nothing to do but wait and concentrate her entire being on drawing the child deep into her consciousness.

It had not been difficult. The powers of *purusha* and *prakriti* would find their way to each other no matter how difficult the circumstance or how impossible the odds. And he was her own son and like with his father, their hearts would always beat as one.

She had been present when he had tamed the elements, reducing Agni, Vayu and Ganga to his playthings as they gambolled across endless space borne along by the Destroyer's might before Mother Earth had risen to hold him close against her bosom. She bore witness to the pain and pleasure that had wracked them all before they received salvation at the hands of the divine prodigy. She had been there every step of the way on the journey he had undertaken so far. She had been there even though she hadn't.

When the Ganas came to Parvati with the happy tidings of the discovery of her son, they were merely telling her what she already knew. They had told her that there was six of him. 'Six that they can see handicapped as they are by the limitations of the gross senses,' she mused to herself, but knew there were so many more. Enough to outnumber the stars in the sky, drops of water in the sea and grains of sand combined. For he had emerged from infinity, the endless, unfathomable source of the divine life force itself.

It was time. Shiva and Parvati set out to meet their son, accompanied by the Ganas. The atmosphere was charged with the excitement and exultation in all their hearts. Shiva smiled when he saw the eager anticipation on his consort's lovely features, which she hadn't bothered to conceal from him and her naked longing tugged at his own heart. To his surprise, he himself was looking forward to meeting the little one who had caused such a ruckus on the occasion of his birth and long before that. In fact, he was feeling a tad nervous at the thought of meeting his son. Shiva hoped his wife would be too distracted to notice.

'It was a good thing the Kartikas took charge of our offspring, wouldn't you say?' he addressed his wife. 'You don't have breasts enough to feed them all.'

Parvati looked at him knowingly but still couldn't resist taking the bait. 'I am perfectly capable of feeding not just our son, but all in creation as you very well know. You don't have to make tasteless jokes just because you are scared senseless at the prospect of meeting the boy in case he has inherited every one of your weaknesses and is inclined to beat you bloody for the many times you have erred!'

'Even if that were the case, he will have enough of your strengths to make up for whatever deficits he has incurred on my account. As for beating me bloody, if the boy is blessed with the peaceable disposition and gentle manner I am known for, it is most unlikely. Besides thanks to his inherited wisdom, he will know better than to do battle with his own blood,' he told her in his most placating manner. 'The Kartikas have done us a great service by taking up such a grave responsibility and discharging their duty with so much merit. They must be rewarded.'

'I am not sure they truly deserve the rewards of the three-eyed God and his especial way of repaying those who have served him in good stead,' Parvati retorted drily. 'From what the Ganas have told me, they were set upon by their husbands who are supposed to be steeped in wisdom but couldn't possibly have been more petty or short-sighted had they tried. They attacked their blameless wives with the intention to kill, abused them most foully and cursed them for good measure. Fie on the lot of them!'

'But the sages did do the right thing by their wives. Thanks to their feckless actions, the Kartikas are no longer bound to the suffocating confines of holy matrimony.' He smiled with pleasure when his wife responded yet again to the provocation and stopped in her tracks to glare at him.

'What I meant was that our son's adoptive mothers do not deserve to be with those who do not appreciate their worth and are better off without their undeserving husbands. Instead they can roam the three worlds wild and free as the wind, going wherever the fates see fit to lead them.' Shiva hastened to add with exaggerated sincerity. 'Besides, their hearts have always belonged to another.'

'The Kartikas have nevertheless lost the security and the other comforts of a domesticated existence. And they will certainly long for the drudgery and monotony they had formerly loathed in the bland landscape of their lives simply because they have been banished and will have to live outside the realms of civilization,' Parvati told him.

Shiva shrugged, 'It is not possible to love and be loved in return without sacrifice. And you are mistaken, my dear! I do believe that they will gladly pay any price that is required of them to serve the one they have given their hearts to.' They stayed silent for a few moments each caught up in their own thoughts. 'You are not thinking of killing them, are you?' he enquired suddenly. 'Along with Agni, Vayu and Ganga?'

His wife's patience was wearing thin and she did not bother with a reply. Besides they were drawing close and she could feel her pulse quickening with pleasurable expectation.

The Kartikas were also aware of their presence and were far from delighted at what they saw as a further encroachment, on what had formerly been a tranquil paradise till their husbands had so rudely trespassed and shattered their happiness. Why couldn't their joy have lasted forever? They read the lament in each other's eyes as well as a grim resolve. Not only would they fight but kill rather than give up what was theirs.

Yet it was hopeless and they knew it. Already the object of their very reason for existence was slipping away, faster than they could muster the strength to hold on. Ever since their six little infants had merged into a single sturdy child, they had known, that the Divine Mother would come to claim him. But even so, they did not want to let go.

Banding around him, the sisters readied themselves for war. Their charge seemed enthused at the prospect of a good fight and he bunched his fists together, bouncing on the balls of his feet, eyes alight with a feverish glow. When the Ganas approached, they hissed in warning, everything about their formidable mien seeming to suggest that if anybody dared to take the boy away from them, there would have a lot more to worry about than cracked skulls and broken bones.

Sensing their belligerence, responding almost by reflex to the heady prospect of violence, the Ganas responded in kind, unsheathing their weapons, brandishing their clubs and hurling vulgar epithets at the warlike women who confronted them. Already they were looking forward to humbling the pride of the viragoes and forcing them to submit, anticipating the ways in which they would force them to yield.

Parvati was furious. She had not envisioned scooping up her son from a sea of blood which was what would most certainly happen if the Ganas were to attack the Kartikas. The anger emanated off her flower-like body in sparks of red. She glared at her husband's followers, allowing her withering scorn to build up from deep within her, feeling it gather force, building on its own momentum as it flooded her being and spilled out in a copious rush, taking the form of strange and frightening creatures who caused the Ganas to scatter pell-mell in fright.

'You may want to give your attendants a lesson in manners,' she admonished her Lord. Shiva wasn't listening. His gaze was fastened on his son and to his wife's utter disbelief, he looked awed. Tenderness suffused her person. You could tell they were father and son. It was there in the way the little boy looked back at the three-eyed God without flinching. The way his eyebrows came together in a straight line when his passions grew stormy. And the tremendous strength and effortless majesty with which he carried himself. Parvati could not bear to look away from that dear, dear face so like her beloved's but fresher and not yet ravaged by time, experience or pain. Hope bloomed in her heart as the future loomed in his countenance, bright with promise.

Her boy peeked at her from behind the Kartikas who were clustered protectively around him and at that moment, she was filled with wonder that her heart could know such profound love for one other than Shiva. When the little one smiled at her in response to the love he sensed she bore him, her joy knew no bounds. At that moment, she knew that there was nothing she wouldn't do for him. Forever more, he would hold the foremost position in her heart.

This raw display of emotion seemed to infuriate and sadden the sisters. They glared at the celestial couple through their tears with ill-concealed dislike and shouted a warning when Parvati took Shiva by the arm in a protective gesture and drew closer to them.

'Stay back,' they spoke in one voice, 'he is all we have and death will claim us before we let you take him away from us!'

'You have sacrificed much for him…' Parvati began.

'What sacrifice? It is a rare privilege to have him in our lives! You couldn't possibly comprehend our feelings which you merely pretend to understand!'

'All I know is that I have lost him once,' she said, her voice choked with tears. 'And I am destined to lose him again. For he will always belong to everybody and yet nobody can claim him for their very own. Yet I live for the brief spell that has been allotted to me. He will be in my arms till it is time for him to go where he must. This cannot be taken away from me.' She finished with a simple irrevocability that crushed the sisters.

With every word she uttered, the Kartikas felt their indomitable spirits quail. They huddled closer to their charge, seeking to memorize the feel of that little body, its perennial warmth which had been such a source of comfort to them. The precious little thing seemed distressed by this excessive and unbecoming display of grief and wailed plaintively to register his protest.

That did it. His happiness would always be paramount to them. Hugging him as one, for the last time, the Kartikas placed the divine child in the outstretched arms of his parents. Parvati turned to them gratefully and was immediately stricken by their heartbreak. 'He will not forget you,' she reassured them. 'Neither will we.'

Shiva nodded, too overcome to speak, as the Kartikas stood before them nearly prostrate with grief.

'May your light shine ever bright and chase away the darkness in whichever corner of the three worlds you choose to inhabit,' Parvati blessed them with all the fervour her overflowing heart could muster. 'Someday my son will come back for you and will bestow his own blessings on the mothers who took such good care of him.'

There was nothing more to be said. The Kartikas made ready to depart, left with little more than memories and the fervent hope that he would call for them. Soon. Not that it mattered. They would spend the aeons ready to serve whenever he needed them. They turned back one last time. 'What will you call him?', they whispered.

'He will be known by many names by those who love him and his parents both, but to us, he will always be Kartikeya.'

Resisting the Resistance

At PARVATI'S INSISTENCE, Kartikeya was whisked away to the upper reaches of Kailash, where the three of them could enjoy some peace and quiet. He played with the snakes in his father's matted locks on the way thither and seemed fascinated by his blue throat and the rivulets of water that flowed sinuously across the length and breadth of his body. Parvati took him in her arms and held him nestled against her own bosom, mildly resentful that he was so deeply enamoured of his father's more odious ornaments.

Their time with their firstborn was precious, Parvati knew, and she was grateful for every moment they had together. It had taken time to adjust to the added addition to their family. Karti's energy levels seemed to dwarf even Shiva's and she found it extraordinarily hard to keep up with him as he tore all over the place in gay abandon getting into all sorts of trouble. In trying to keep up with him, her luscious mane became every bit as messy as Shiva's and her body as begrimed as the two males in her life.

Hardest of all was to find a private moment with Shiva so that they could resume their lovemaking. Karti insisted on having their combined attention all to himself. When they succeeded in stealing away together, he decided that there was no pastime in the three worlds more diverting than time spent with his parents and screamed himself hoarse till they came for him.

'Perhaps it is his way of letting us know that he does not want a little brother or sister,' Shiva told her exasperatedly.

'Would you like to make another baby?' Parvati asked him softly.

'I would love to have a little girl...' Shiva was saying when Karti came tearing into their presence and squeezed himself between them.

'I would prefer a bear,' he interjected, 'they are better than girls to play with. A tawny lion wouldn't be too bad either.'

His parents looked at each other over his head and smiled. 'Why don't you go play with Nandi...' Shiva urged him.

'Nandi is boring and tells me the same stories over and over again. I know them all by heart.'

Karti was almost as trying as his father, Parvati decided, but still, there were moments with him that were so magical, she felt like the luckiest being in all of creation. She enjoyed taking care of her boy and loved the way he always came running to her for a hug or quick cuddle no matter how busily he was otherwise engaged. But best of all was the way Shiva responded to him.

Father and son could play together forever, it seemed. Her husband seemed to have become a boy again, leapfrogging across the snowy heights of Kailash, bombarding them all with snowballs and racing past his son as they swam across Lake

Manasarovar, who in turn would become incensed not only because his father had beat him but because he was cognizant of her frantic signals to Shiva, urging him to let Kartikeya win. Her Lord even threw tantrums every bit as fierce as Karti's when it appeared that he might lose at some of the complicated games they made up which usually involved a lot of roughhousing. 'What a pair they make!' she mused fondly, gazing at her special boys.

They also had the longest conversations about practically everything under the sun. Sometimes it was about silly things such as facial hair and the sage who explained away his noisy flatulence by saying that it was quietly expelled wind that smelled the worst (the two laughed themselves silly over this instance of scatological gold).

At other times, they spoke about the mysteries of the universe, or, as she observed wryly when she heard some of their fancier notions, what they understood of it anyway. There was also the time she heard her son explain the significance of *Om* to his father.

Shiva had swelled with pride and bequeathed him with the grave responsibility of educating his followers on Earth as well. It was Karti's turn to puff up with self-importance at his father's trust in him. Parvati loved them both so much it hurt. She fervently wished that things would stay the same forever.

The Devas, of course, wished otherwise. They had arranged a grand reception for their saviour with Indra and Brahma at their head. Nandi told them all about it, while Kartikeya played with his horns and pulled his tail. 'They want the God of Gods to crown their deliverer and formally appoint him as the Commander-in-Chief of the celestial army. On Indra's orders, they have depleted Kubera's secret store of fabled treasures to create a throne and crown worthy of your son.' He stopped short, when Parvati snorted loudly to indicate her contempt. If he hadn't worshipped the ground she walked on, he would have judged her behaviour most unladylike.

Shiva nodded at him, encouraging him to continue. 'Brahma and the *saptarishis* have assembled as well. They want to perform his sacred thread ceremony to the accompaniment of Vedic chants and anoint him with the waters of the holy rivers that they have gathered and consecrated with the power of their devotional hymns and *mantras*.'

This time it was Shiva who snorted. It was an explosive sound which made Nandi jump. What were they thinking? He and his wife were simple ascetics who lived in the wild, at one with the elements, clad in animal skins, content to put as much distance as was possible from the men and Gods alike with their obsession for power and all its trappings, even as they did their duty by them. And yet they sought to woo his son and convince him to champion their cause with filthy lucre and a whole lot of decorative baubles.

Perhaps they had forgotten the days when he and Kali quaffed intoxicants enough to drown the three worlds in, danced and made love so violently, the extraordinary energy released by their frenzied coupling had threatened to destroy the three worlds. Now that Shiva was a householder, they probably figured he would go the whole hog and embrace the very things that had long enslaved them.

Nandi was still speaking, 'They are all eager to bestow valuable gifts on Shiva's son, in addition to the honours that go with the exalted rank of the *Senapati* of the Devas, of course. Brahman will imbue him with Vedic knowledge painstakingly gathered over the aeons and offer him the use of his own

Brahmastra. Varuna will offer him the hidden treasures of the seas. A chariot swifter than thought will be Surya's gift and Kubera will shower down all of his fabled treasures on him in addition to giving him the *antardhana*. Kama's power of love and desire will forever flavour his existence. Even the Goddesses compete with each other to give him the best presents—from wealth and prosperity to wisdom.'

He paused to take a breath, before continuing, 'Indra will part with his mighty *vajra* and offer him the finest war elephants sired by his Airavata. In addition to that, he is determined that Shiva's son, whom he strongly believes is the fruition of the prayers of the Devas and the sum total of every worthy act they have ever performed over the *kalpas*, must be united to him by familial bonds. Devendra offers the hand of his exquisite daughter...'

Parvati had heard enough. It was bad enough that she had to share Shiva with all who would inveigh upon his attention but must she lose her little boy to the first chippie offered as a pawn by those who would do anything to regain power? Besides, Indra's gifts would no doubt be every bit as awful as Indra himself.

'None of them must be allowed anywhere near my son. And that goes doubly so for Indra and his offspring. Throwing him off a cliff would be kinder than getting him married to Indra's odious daughter. What are the Devas thinking, coming here with their demands over and over again just because their King insists?' Her voice rang out with authority, 'The gifts they bear are poisoned and bear the taint of their endless avarice. He is a child and yet they seek to send him into battle against demons and ensnare him with the bond of matrimony which some would attest is even more intolerable! This time around, the Ganas will face my wrath if anyone or anything dares to approach my abode without my approval.'

Nandi bowed deeply before taking his leave of them.

'The gifts are his to accept or spurn,' Shiva chided her, setting aside his own misgivings when faced with the vitriolic strength of her repugnance. 'I don't think much of them either, but to the Devas, they are the most precious things they own. It is simply their way of showing love and respect.'

'That may be the case,' Parvati acceded grudgingly, 'but they are not given freely and come with the burden of terrible expectations. Why should my son stain his hands with the blood of the sons of Maya just so Indra can reclaim a throne he ill deserves? Soora is your devotee and this is not how he should be repaid.'

'Which is all the more reason for my son to put an end to a life he no longer cares for, to release him from the suffocating confines of an existence where peace and contentment elude him, mired as he is in the sticky web of ignorance and illusion. If Indra craves for superficial pleasures and materialistic gain, blinded as he is by his unbridled lust for power, it is exactly what he deserves. You are just scared that things will change faster than you can come to terms with.' *And have no wish to lose your son to another.* Wisely, he did not give voice to that last thought.

'Aren't you?' Parvati glared at him, furious that she was unable to refute his words. 'I thought it would be the two of us together...but it can never be, given how we always seem to be pulled apart in different directions by our diametrically opposed natures. And certainly not with the mortals and immortals clamouring for your attention, a seductress who clings to you like a second skin and your own natural inclination to be forever detached from the demands of a householder's existence, which prompts you to turn inward till you are entombed within your own solitude.'

She was becoming increasingly upset and it was hard to find the right words through her tears. 'I want things to be different for our son. It is my wish that there is more of happiness and less of tumult in his existence. He must not go through the conflict from within and without that tears apart all in existence.'

'It is what every parent wants for their child, but that is not the way of things as you very well know. And, try as you might, you cannot shield him forever from the demands of his very existence. The will of destiny cannot be thwarted and it is futile to fight it. Besides, he is our son, even if the boy is buffeted by the stormy winds of fate and rent asunder, he will emerge again from the ether, stronger than ever before.'

Shiva spoke with all the kindness he could muster even as he wondered how it was that she who possessed so much wisdom could allow herself to be blinded by maternal love.

'What are you talking about?' Kartikeya wanted to know. He clambered into his mother's lap knowing that she needed to be comforted. 'Is it about the Devas and their present difficulties with the Asura brothers?'

'Who told you that?' Parvati wanted to know. Already she was thinking of creative ways to punish the loose-lipped ones among the Ganas who had been blabbing to him of the troubles of the Devas. In her opinion, they did not have it too bad. Soora had spared their lives and chased them away into exile. If only they stopped grieving over the loss of their paltry possessions and precious luxuries, they could make something of themselves, as opposed to being the perpetual nuisance and cringeworthy whiners they were now.

'Nobody, mother,' he answered her truthfully. 'I can hear them. Their voices raise quite the ruckus in my head. They want me to get rid of Soora and his brothers so that they can reclaim the things they firmly believe have been taken from them, the ones they think they cannot possibly do without. They don't realize that Soora is no happier than they are and would gladly give it all up but his ego won't let him simply because he would rather not part with his acquisitions that are so deeply coveted by his enemies.'

Karti had closed his eyes so that he could hear the voices better. 'The Devas seek the death of not only Soora but his brothers as well, Simha and Taraka. They in turn call out to me as well. Soora is filled with disenchantment and the restlessness that drives him to despair has robbed him of the ability to savour the flavours of his existence. All his life, Simha has thirsted for knowledge hoping that it will set him free but the more he learns the less he understands of universal truths. As for Taraka, there has seldom been a creature more tormented by pain. His enmity with Indra, who is guilty of having cruelly abused, tortured and violated one who was most dear to him has been carried over from another age. It has infected him from within and the poison has suppurated his very soul.'

His voice throbbed with passion and intensity as storm clouds gathered on the horizon, dark and filled with foreboding. Parvati frowned at Shiva as though it was his fault that their child wasn't quite a child and already possessed the wisdom of an ancient, forcing him to shoulder responsibilities that were not entirely age-appropriate.

'What else do you hear, son?' Shiva pretended not to notice her ire and turned his full attention to his son.

'Oh! Many things...'

Karti shrugged distractedly, reverting effortlessly to being the child he was, the son his mother wanted to hold and protect. He had gotten his hands on Shiva's *damaru*, enormously pleased that his mother was too upset to take it back and tell him that it was not a toy for him to play with. 'There are two girls whose voices are most insistent and they rise above the general clamour.'

'What do they want?' Parvati asked through clenched teeth.

'Probably something boring or gross,' he stuck out his tongue to convey his disdain for the members of the other sex who followed him around begging to be included in his preferred activities with the Ganas. Not all of them were tiresome, he conceded to himself, especially the ones who enjoyed running wild with the Bhootaganas and Pisachas who made up his father's entourage. But most wanted to play kissing games, and in his opinion, there were plenty of better things to do.

His mother's expression softened as Kartikeya knew it would. For the time being at least, she was the love of his life. He hoped his father wouldn't tell her that the two were Vishnu's daughters and had been betrothed in another life to the sons of Shiva and Shakti. But Daksha's ill-fated *yagna*, which saw Shiva's beloved consign her body to the flames, had put paid to all that. So now the two girls had taken birth to unite themselves to him. Mercifully for his mother, there was a long way to go before all that came to pass and there was no need to distress her unduly at this juncture.

Shiva winked at him conspiratorially, and Karti smiled back at him. 'What do you intend to do about the voices raised to seek your aid, son?' he asked with genuine curiosity.

Parvati held her breath.

'There will come a time when I must attend to them. But that moment is not this one nor the next or the one after. For now, it is time for that rematch you promised me after cheating me of victory by resorting to duplicitous tricks in a manner most unworthy of the greatest of Gods. Now that I have grown wise to them, you haven't a prayer of ever prevailing over me!'

'We will see about that!' Shiva said with gusto. Watching the two of them tear off into the distance, trying to trip one another as they jostled for advantage in one of their endless races, Parvati allowed herself to breathe again.

Setting Off a Chain Reaction

$\mathcal{I}$NDRA WAS BROODING. He felt as though the wheel of time had ground to a halt just to spite him. Despite his unceasing efforts, nothing was happening. It felt as though he had been running with all his might across a harsh and unforgiving landscape for practically forever but next to no progress had been made. If he didn't know better, he'd think he was expending his dwindling strength to run in place. This was exactly the sort of thing that could drive one to despair and ultimately, insanity.

Shiva's son had finally shown up after a whole lot of volatile drama and Indra had allowed himself to hope. He could almost feel the golden throne against his royal backside as he reclined rigidly on its unyielding, uncomfortable surface, basking in the warm afterglow of absolute power. Reflexively, he tried to unclench his buttocks. Soora was still very much around and clearly he was doing all the basking.

In fact, his informers had told him that his adversary

had been cool as you please and celebrated the birth of his favourite God's son by ordering celebrations across the length and breadth of his kingdom, instead of commissioning the customary decorous pujas to mark the occasion. He had banned the performance of *yagnas,* which had formerly been conducted with such pomp and splendour in order to invoke the favour of the Devas, and locked away the priests who had long upheld the Vedic way of life accusing them of thievery for having charged exorbitant rates to mouth mumbo jumbo, while offering endless libations to insatiable Agni and daring to 'malign meat'.

Many among his subjects had actually lauded his actions! There were some fanatical creatures who worshipped Soora as a God and had built shrines in his honour. The worship conducted in these so-called holy places usually involved drinking, dancing, feasting on animal flesh and the active pursuit of carnal passion. The whole thing was a vulgar reversal of the traditional rites and rituals so lovingly safeguarded by the Devas. It had really gotten to Indra. Perhaps such blind fools truly deserved the likes of Soora to lord it over them.

Thanks to the largesse of the tyrant and his perverse decision to commemorate the birth of his slayer, his subjects had gorged themselves fit to burst on meat and wine aplenty. Soora's underlings had slaughtered every animal they could get their hands on—chickens, goats, boars, hippos, elephants and even sacred cows—offering it all to the masses maddened by the lust for meat.

During his reign, encouraged by the priests and with Indra's approval, many had taken up vegetarianism, which anybody with sense would know was the key to health and long life. Soora, however, had declared that such a notion was fool's talk and if all were to embrace vegetarianism, the three worlds would be stripped of green cover and overrun with beasts and birds if they were left unconsumed on a regular basis.

The poor, who normally subsisted on grain, had swarmed over the carcasses like an army of ants, armed with sharp implements, helping themselves to blood, fat and flesh, chewing and swallowing with gusto, sometimes eating even the offal raw because they were too impatient to roast it on hastily made cooking fires.

Soon they were all covered in the blood, gore, excrement and digestive juices of the poor creatures they had slain, rubbing their stuffed bellies with an air of contentment. Barrels of wine were brought forth and the great, unwashed masses ululated with joy as they drank themselves into a leaden stupor. Almost immediately the celebrations devolved into a combination of drinking, dancing and the debauched indulgence of the rank desires of the flesh.

Indra could see the scenes of feasting and abundant lovemaking, almost as if he had been there, watching. It made him sick to the stomach. The way he saw it, this sort of untrammelled wantonness mirrored the moral morass the three words had succumbed to ever since Soora had taken the reins of power in his grubby paws. It is known that the mortals take their cues from their betters. With the hedonistic and animalistic brothers at the helm, the humans had sunk into an abyss of sin and thoughtless self-indulgence. If he, as the upholder of truth and virtue, did nothing to treat the rot that had taken root on Bhoomi Devi in the form of his accursed nemesis, it would be the end of them all.

Feeling impossibly pious and heroic, Indra went to meet his wife, the redoubtable Sachidevi, whose thoughts usually mirrored his own, a fitting quality for a dutiful wife to have. She too tended to preoccupy herself with the foibles of greater humanity and was a fanatical subscriber to the belief that the only way to destroy evil was to go after the vessels that carried the slightest hint of it, without exception or mercy. Especially when they stood in the way of her reclaiming her status as Queen.

Suddenly he felt a pang. Could it be guilt? 'It is not like I am doing something untoward,' he assured himself. 'All I am going to do is tell her a story and send her on a little trip with our son for company. Plus a handpicked coterie of his personal bodyguards who had a mostly ill-deserved reputation for unthinking brutality. And if their paths crossed with a certain accursed creature who would be the spark that set off an almighty conflagration, surely no one in the right mind would blame me, would they?'

─❦─

Soora had decided to take a little trip himself, with Simha for company. For obvious reasons he was morbidly fascinated with the one who it had been foretold would slay Maya's sons. He had expected Simha to resist his plan to make the journey that would allow them to take a gander at Shiva's son but his brother had been almost as keen. By mutual consent, they decided to leave Taraka to his own devices. Neither of them wished for him to add strangling or attempting to strangle a little boy to his burgeoning list of transgressions.

Leaving the cares of running an empire behind and feeling very much like two mischievous boys up to no good, they set off to the very heights of Kailash. Soora was disguised as a bloodthirsty vampire. He looked positively fiendish with blood dripping off his sharpened teeth and took considerable pleasure every time passers-by took to their heels at the sight of him. Simha was in the guise of a diseased beggar. Having worked with the dregs of society for a while now, he was confident that he could pass off as one.

'You look atrocious and stink to the high heavens,' Soora jibed, 'but that said, this is a considerable improvement on your unspeakably unfortunate looks and lack of physical charm!'

'Jealousy is your worst attribute, brother,' his brother countered. 'I wish you would just make your peace with the fact that I am the best looking of Maya's sons and certainly the most leonine in countenance as well as conduct!'

'You wish!' Soora shouted holding his sides as he erupted in laughter, his mirth scaring the birds off the trees. 'Lion-faced, indeed! Actually, your grotesque mien resembles the unwashed hindquarters of the great beasts!'

'I have missed this,' Simha told him seriously, scratching at a pustule on his bottom vigorously. 'Life used to be a lot simpler when I was hanging suspended by my toes, Taraka was carving out slices of his body to offer to Shiva, and you stood in the midst of the *panchagni*, impervious to the crackling of your roasting flesh, the sound of which distracted me from my own pain, when we went the distance to accrue glory to our names.'

'We were such morons,' his brother exclaimed, caught up in the true spirit of nostalgia. 'It is too bad Mother forgot to tell us that getting your heart's desire is oftentimes the worst thing that can happen to you! And sometimes all the effort and hard work expended in the pursuit of glory is almost not worth it. Wouldn't it have been something if she had allowed us to remain mediocre beings with no greater ambition than to have food in our bellies, clothes on our backs, a roof over our heads and a woman to live unhappily ever after with?'

'Don't let Taraka hear you questioning our sainted mother's more dubious decisions,' Simha replied, only half in jest. 'But if you could actually go back in time, would you make things different?'

'Of course not! This is my life and I am determined to be proud of it, even if it is hopelessly abysmal on the best of days. But still, we should have had the sense to ask that we be turned into unfeeling rocks content to repose side by side for all off eternity while the elements have their way with us and the birds shit on our sorry selves.'

Simha wasn't entirely sure his brother was joking so he laughed extra hard to mask his uncertainty as well as the ever-present uneasiness. Together, they joined the singularly ranks of those who thronged to see the Destroyer in the hopes of deliverance or the chance to get hopelessly drunk and dance away their troubles. The destitute, deformed, disabled, deprived, disgusting, dispossessed and deceived, as well as those who sought to deceive, were all welcome in Shiva's realm. He was happy to receive the misfits, miscreants, misshapen and miserable who were not wanted anywhere else in the world.

It was what had drawn Maya's sons to the Destroyer in the first place. The brothers were surprised at how well they fit in and how much the raucous revelry suited them. Embracing all things depraved and debauched somehow had a curiously liberating effect and seemed to let them transcend the limitations of a spirit that had been bogged down by vice and virtue alike.

'I knew there was a reason I have a soft spot for the Destroyer,' Soora whispered to his brother, 'even knowing that his brat has every intention of pulling out my entrails and hanging me with it.'

Almost as if he had heard, the object of their thoughts materialized in the midst of the devotees. He was an impossibly handsome child with luscious curls which bounced off his well-formed shoulders, eyes that sparkled with boundless energy and mirth, and a golden countenance. Like his father, he showed no revulsion for the more unfortunate of the faithful as they gathered around him in a mad rush knocking those who got in the way underfoot. Ghouls and goblins swarmed towards him shrieking and snarling fit to wake the dead and derange the damned as all fought to get closer to Shiva's son. To imbibe a portion of the essence that imbued the child born with the divine spark.

Soora and Simha threw themselves into the unfolding chaos with unabashed gusto, thrusting aside caution and civilized conduct, knocking heads while wielding the blades and axes that had somehow come into their possession with unerring skill. Soon they were bathed in blood and picking out fragments of bone from their teeth and dishevelled garments, wading through the sea of bodies, giving as good as they got.

Madness coupled frenetically with mayhem, driving them into a wild frenzy as they wallowed in death and destruction, toiling in the midst of turmoil, unable to resist the siren call of savagery. Hacking and bludgeoning their way ever deeper into the heart of the mob, they cracked skulls by the dozens, plunging their blades into soft, naked flesh, revelling in the sight of spilled grey matter and flesh that had already begun to spoil. This was raw power and they grew engorged on it, in the absence of all checks and balances. If this was what it took to draw as close as it was possible to the divine person of the Destroyer's son, perhaps even merge into his exalted being, they would gladly pay the price. With interest.

Tantalizing glimpses of the boy inundated their senses. A flash of those beguiling eyes that brimmed over with mischief though their depths hinted at the ocean of knowledge they contained. Lustrous runaway curls that almost brushed across the bloodied welts of their forearms, dimpled elbows that nearly grazed their ribs which seemed to have been staved in by unfriendly clubs wielded with ferocious intent. But it was all worth it when they finally collapsed at the feet of the one who was known by many names, spent and utterly drained. It could have been a reward for their exertions...the unwelcome intrusion of his followers vanished into the distance.

It was hard to say if any of it was real, although it most certainly felt that way. More so than anything they had experienced before. Or would after. It was equally possible that they were dreaming or trapped in the inhospitable terrain of an inescapable nightmare. Neither could be certain if they wished to leave at once or remain for all of eternity. Was it undiluted pleasure they were experiencing or the worst pain imaginable? Later, all that stayed with them was the experience or what they could remember of it, since neither of them would have agreed on the details if they had ever chosen to talk about it. Not that any of it mattered in the least. Or perhaps it did. It was impossible to tell.

They had caught on fire. But it did not burn even when it consumed them entirely. The flames coursed through their veins, scorching their hearts, filling them with incandescent light that lit up every cell, every infinitesimal part of their very minds and bodies.

Many were the things they saw. And there was so much more which they couldn't see. Nor did they wish to.

There was fighting. A lot of it. Men cheering themselves hoarse as cocks fought to the death. The fowls fought other cocks and eagles which were fighting yet more eagles in an exhilarating enterprise that was most foul. Peacocks feasted on an abundant supply of writhing snakes and twisting serpents, obliging the exhortations of the cheering spectators baying for blood. Encouraged towards greater exertions, the eerily beautiful birds employed their unnaturally sharpened talons to rake and rend, till their brilliant plumages glistened with every shade of crimson. It was tear or be torn apart.

Yet, the watchers wanted more. Ever more. Disgruntled when the birds failed to deliver the cheap thrills they lived for, necks were wrung and lifeless bodies, magnificent even after death were discarded, tossed carelessly into a great, depthless pit filled to the brim with corpses.

Even as they watched from the comfort of a great distance, the brothers knew that they were a part of the macabre monstrosities they had somehow engineered. What unholy force had driven them to do it? What discernible purpose did such damnable callousness serve? All around there was shouting and screaming. They wanted it to stop until they realized it was their own shrieks of abject despair. Even that realization did not make it stop.

The brothers clung to each other for dear life but the gale forces of destruction that buffeted them from all sides was having none of it and they were torn asunder into a million pieces to be cast adrift on the tides of oblivion. Never to be recovered.

But it wasn't the end. Not for Soora. Nor his dreams. He had performed the most intense of tapas over the aeons, subjecting his physical body to extreme agony. So great was his need. He would have stopped at nothing and he didn't. When the impossible was granted to him, and the King could have whatever his heart desired, he realized *that he did not want any of the things he had wanted badly enough to die for. So he asked only that he be allowed to serve and do something, anything at all that actually mattered. Whatever that may entail. In whatever form. Be it a peacock or a cock or a marauding elephant bearing its Lord into battle.*

Who was he? The wise King who had wanted everything but made the decision to settle for nothing. The wind whispered its secret swallowing it up as quickly as it was said. But he heard. A name. Prabhakara. It had been his own name, Soora knew. From a time before memory.

Simha floundered like one lost at sea as the tides dragged him hither and thither. There was a girl. There always was a girl. There was the violation of free will. A lion savaging its prey. Giving free rein to a ferocious appetite, digesting the chewed out remains of the rights of another. There was blood running in copious streams over limbs locked together in hopeless protest and a vile perpetrator's will was sealed by every ruby red drop that drenched Mother Earth. There was the promise of retribution. Tempered with hope. Even atonement. Before salvation.

Anguish and remorse tore through them. It was too much. More than they could withstand; more than anybody could withstand. The relentless onslaught of brutal truth could not be borne. Stop! Please stop! For the love of all things holy, STOP!

And it did.

All that remained was a dear face, an impossibly beautiful one wreathed in compassion. And a promise so pure it could have only been uttered by a child. 'You are not ready. But you will be. We will meet again when you are. It will get worse before it gets better. Then you can choose to stay by my side. Even if it is forever. Or as long as it matters.'

The brothers found themselves back where they had started. Buoyed and alert for the battle ahead. They knew that they must submit to the almighty force they had experienced which they hadn't begun to understand. But not before they fought the good fight. For so it must be.

A Linga Bathed in Blood

𝒾T WAS THE crudest of shrines, if it could even be called that. A humble Shiva Linga fashioned out of stone stood on a small altar beneath a massive tree. The more diminutive of its woody brethren in the vicinity had been torn down to create a small clearing. That was about all the effort that had gone into the making of this abode for God. Yet somehow it had caught the fancy of the faithful and devotees belonging to all species made the difficult journey to the sacred relic through extremely inhospitable forest terrain, bringing whatever they could scrounge up by way of offerings.

At any given time of the day, the Linga was festooned with faded flowers, chewed-up fruits, gourds filled with milk and bloody bits of raw meat that remained untouched till the animal denizens of the land waited for the humans to make themselves scarce and helped themselves to all things edible, in the Lord's name, of course. This had the somewhat unfortunate result of dried up faeces of unknown origin, bird as well as animal droppings dotting the immediate surroundings of the symbol of Mahadeva.

Aja (only her mother used her full name, Ajamukhi), liked it better than any other place in the three worlds and was known to repair there from time to time. She could spend days there, subsisting on the delicious packed meals some of the devotees who, irrespective of whether they knew her or not, kindly shared with her. It was her practice to sit there thinking of nothing, or to let her thoughts wander where they would.

Her brothers simply could not comprehend how she could possibly turn her back on the new-found opulence that was theirs to enjoy and give up her right to wallow in the lap of luxury after all the privations they had endured. But she hadn't expected them to.

Their mother's grandiose dreams fuelled by anger and hatred nursed across endless generations over countless lifetimes had never held much appeal for her. Aja preferred to follow in the steady footsteps of her father, the great Sage Kashyapa, and devote herself to the sedate exploration of universal truths deep in the forests which were their home. Like him, she was given to wandering wherever her feet saw fit to take her, as time carried her faraway on its tides. Much of her time was spent in silent contemplation and in the stillness, her mind travelled through the ether into places where none before her had been. It wasn't exactly a glorious enterprise which she had undertaken, filled with endless adventure, marvellous wonders and fresh insights.

Mostly it was all mundane and she felt that no matter where she went or what she did everything was exactly the same. It was like going around in circles. Even breaking the pattern was starting to feel like a pattern. Aja didn't exactly love the life she was living but the important thing was that she did not hate it. She liked to think that she took after her father. Yet the exact same attributes which had made him so revered led to her being reviled.

All were convinced that she was idling away time when she could have just as easily done her duty by marrying and bringing forth a brood of brats. This unanimous belief led to others equally spurious where it was surmised that those who whiled away the daylight hours did so because they were most likely fatigued from nights spent labouring away on one's back or knees or in other unseemly positions that their imaginations could conjure. Yet those whose paths crossed with hers couldn't help noticing that the plain face was always aglow with a strange light, which could hardly be called telltale evidence of vice.

Many were drawn to Aja or that undefinable thing that she exuded and they gravitated towards her hoping to be bathed in the same radiance. It had to be confessed that Aja herself did not exactly welcome the company, even if she liked a few of them well enough. They all seemed to want to keep her close to them but all she could do was share a little warmth and laughter before moving on. It made her irresistible to even more of those she would rather avoid.

The bizarre magnetism was attributed to the rumour that she was both a whore and a witch. These were things that were uttered in hushed voices for Ajamukhi or 'Goat face', as she was called, was the sister of a tyrant, corrupt crook and monster. Many would have liked to have her pinioned beneath a strong knee or thrown in chains so that the immoral wretch could be taught a lesson. But none dared do so.

It would never do to molest a wanton witch who, in

addition to having powerful brothers with an extraordinary capacity for violence, was the possessor of black arts, the whispers claimed. Those in the 'know' or believed themselves to be insisted that her preferred pastime was sucking the blood and soul out of every male organ that caught her lascivious eye, leaving only the desiccated corpse behind for carrion crows to feed on.

That one had made Aja laugh. Taraka had thought it funny too. Or he pretended to. It was hard to tell with him. His victims, the ones accused of casting slurs on his beloved sister failed to see the humour in the situation and would have been hard pressed to smile, with their chopped genitals stuffed into their mouths.

When she found out, Aja had refused to talk to her brother. He had taken it badly, for he was inordinately fond of her despite the fact that she was the only one who pulled him up every time she deemed his actions unconscionable. Sulking and raging like a child, his fury was a thing to behold but his temper, which made battle-hardened veterans wet themselves, left her unmoved. Ultimately though, he had desisted from relieving those accused of bad-mouthing his sister of their genitalia. Only then had she deigned to stay with him at Shonitpur for a while and he had gone out of his way to do nothing to incur her displeasure, keeping her close to him at all times.

All that had been a while ago but from what Aja had heard, Taraka's personal demons continued to thrive on all the messy things he had no doubt inherited from mother, while Soora and Simha indulged him because neither could bring themselves to talk some sense into his head. Aja missed them. For all their faults, they were her brothers and she loved them and would do so even if they stood accused of strangling kittens and setting blind old women on fire.

She did not care to be a part of their world, though. The solitude and tranquillity of her chosen existence was exactly what she wanted for herself and Aja would not have traded it for anything at all.

Every once in a while, she returned to her childhood home for reasons even she did not quite understand. It wasn't too far from where she was seated but the forests had reclaimed it a long time ago. All that remained was the dear misshapen Linga she was inexplicably drawn to. It was pleasant to repose there, thinking and reflecting, though she could and did do just that everywhere else as well.

Maya could have forgiven her for being a whoring witch but she simply could not condone a child of hers turning out to be a wandering wastrel. She had never had much use for her daughter especially since she had been blessed with three strong sons who did exactly as they were told but the matriarch found it bitterly galling that Aja did not have much use for her either. What was worse, the little strumpet was more than a match even for her mother's formidable will and no amount of threatening, thrashing or tempting could convince her to be a pawn in Maya's power games.

'You are a disobedient child and an ingrate! Those who are foolhardy and insist on thwarting a mother's will are doubly cursed,' Maya had spat out after a bitter spat. 'I tell you with every fibre of my being that you will come to a terrible end! Disgrace and infamy will be your lot! When death pries you away, the regret that will burn your soul will be of great comfort to me in the afterlife!'

'So be it, Mother!' she had replied stony-eyed and white-faced. 'Not even the prospect of the horrors you wish for me will deter me from living my life as I see fit. There is no threat you could utter that would make me foolish enough to squander away precious time by chasing after poisoned dreams that involve war mongering and large-scale destruction.'

'Would you rather make love instead?' her mother barked. 'Is whoring your true calling? Had I known that you were so disgustingly weak I would have exposed you to the elements at birth and left you to die!'

For a sore moment Aja was tempted to reply in kind. But the violence in her mother's words was even worse than that in Soora's wars and she refused to be party to it. There was nothing more to be said. The only good thing she could take away from her odious relationship with her mother was the comforting knowledge that she was doing the right thing if only because Maya was so vehemently opposed to her way of life. Prostrating herself at her mother's feet in mock obeisance, she had turned and walked away.

Aja hadn't looked back since. Until today. Her mind refused to allow her to dwell on the implications of the terrible things that had been said on that day. She had nearly forgotten about it, but seated before the Linga she remembered. And wished she hadn't.

Besides she had come here to remonstrate with the Destroyer. Aja had loved him all her life but sometimes his conduct was beyond maddening. She frowned at the Linga. *Whatever do you mean by creating a son to kill my brothers?* The words were addressed to the three-eyed God from the private sanctuary of her mind. She knew that he heard her even though he insisted on pretending he was deaf and dumb.

Soora has a good heart as you very well know! He has his flaws

but they are certainly not as numerous as your own. Leave him be!
Simha is a dear and only a madman would wish to harm him! Taraka
can be a bit of a monster but that is true of every one of the male
species without exception and there is much that is good in him. Don't
you dare hurt my brothers or you will have me to answer to! Do you
hear?

Silence assailed her eardrums. Her breathing had grown
heavy and she tried to calm herself down. Sometimes Shiva was
so trying! If she envied her brothers one thing, it was that they
had been blessed enough to have actually seen the three-eyed
God. Aja had wept for days when they had refused to take her
along, believing that she was too delicate to make the arduous
journey to meet the Destroyer. They never spoke to anybody
about their tryst with the three-eyed God.

All she knew was that it had changed them somehow;
made them over into beings who were being borne along by a
mighty force that lesser men would never have withstood. In
her heart, she knew that they had been chosen for something
special. It had made her feel left out and for the longest time she
visited the Linga to rail at it.

Yet there were other days when she did not believe any of
it and she entertained a dark suspicion that Mother had given
her brothers one of her potions to delude them into thinking
that Shiva, so far removed from the petty struggles of a sordid,
mundane existence, had granted them his favour. Perhaps it had
all been a hallucination…a fever dream that had toppled Indra's
reign.

Now the wheel of time had turned and there was talk
about a six-headed baby who had emerged from Shiva's seed
charged by the power of his *tapas*. They said the child had
been forged by the destructive power of Mahadeva and was not

tempered by the temperate juices in Parvati's womb. He was supposedly the perfect weapon made for the express purpose of shedding blood. Her brothers' in particular.

An old woman began to sing a hymn. A few others joined their voices to hers. They were people from all walks of life and here, in their shared love of Mahadeva, they saw fit to cast their differences aside. Aja listened in silence. She loved the vibrations here. It was so peaceful and made her feel like she had entered a safe haven. Every time she got into a tiff with her mother, it had been her practice to retire to this very spot. In here, she felt there was always hope.

Yet, this time around there was something in the air, a certain heaviness that made her more than a little uneasy. It was still, uncomfortably so, almost as if the elements were holding their breath. Waiting and watching. For whatever it was that was coming. She brushed the fanciful notion away impatiently and forced her thoughts to return to her brothers.

While she had embarked on her seemingly aimless journeys that took her far away so that she could get closer to herself, Soora, Simha, Taraka and the three worlds had lurched along, stumbling blindly into catastrophes of their own making. Aja thought fondly of her big brother, who had dared to risk his mother's wrath by refusing to treat her with anything other than absolute affection.

'Why can't you be a good girl and marry someone of your choosing? Or someone whom Mother would have approved off?' Soora had pleaded with her, shortly after Maya's passing. 'You broke her heart with your steady refusals and she would rest easier knowing that you have settled down.'

'You know as well as I do that Mother did not have a heart,' she had retorted. 'Why would you try to force marriage on me when yours has been such a spectacular failure? Despite being the wife of the all-powerful monarch of the three worlds, not many even know her name, because there are too many women in your life for even those who are obsessed with your every move to keep track of them all! All your women seem content to forget their troubles by distracting themselves with the baubles of your exalted position and have resignedly sacrificed everything they are and could be on the altar of your ego!'

'It is not the worst way to live...' he began, amused and awed as ever by her fearlessness in addressing him thus. Not even Simha or Taraka had her courage. What a King she would have made!

'It is certainly the best way to die even when you are still alive,' she dead-panned. 'Simha does his best, but his simpering wife isn't worth the wind he breaks so frequently, and don't even get me started on Taraka! From what I hear, he holds the noble institution of marriage foisted on us by those Devas in even more contempt than I do but he gave in to Mother's wishes and married that timid, long-suffering nincompoop who put up with his attentions long enough to bear him three sons before dying and abandoning them all. Now those poor boys have no buffer to shield them from the excesses of dear Taraka and...'

'Is that what you are afraid of?' he teased, pretending not to have heard her acute observations on Taraka. 'Death by childbirth? Or the odious "attentions" of your husband? Rest assured, I will drive Yama back with his *danda* up his righteous backside and none among the mortals or immortals would dare to lay a finger on my sister against her will!'

'You know I am afraid of nothing,' she had replied

exasperatedly, 'and I am no shrinking virgin to flee in the face of a man's advances when it is not unsolicited.' To his credit, Soora had never been a hypocrite like their mother and would not judge her. In fact, he admired her refusal to bow down before the demands of conventionality, not that he would admit as much.

When Maya had eased her death grip on life she had extracted a promise from him to do his utmost to straighten out his recalcitrant sister and he felt obliged to make the effort every once in a while. Not that it did any good. Or ever would.

Thinking of Soora's words made her smile. It was how the intruders found her when they barged into her sanctuary.

'Why! If it isn't Ajamukhi, disgraced sister of Soorapadma, the usurper,' an imperious voice rang out, slicing into her thoughts and rudely interrupting the hymn. All of the devout fell silent. Some were already scuttling away towards the relative safety of the surrounding trees, having decided to make a run for it. No good was going to come of this encounter between Soora's sister and Indra's wife who happened to have an armed escort led by her belligerent son, Jayanta.

A daring few hung back watching with morbid fascination, hypnotized by the impending violence that reared its head with the sinuous grace of a striking cobra. A lone figure stole away quietly to converse with another who was waiting for him. He hoped his companion would reach the one who had charged him with keeping a discreet eye on his sister quickly. If anything happened to Ajamukhi, there would be hell to pay, of course. But he knew that something bad *was* going to happen to her. His life would be expended in trying to shield her but it wasn't going to be enough.

'Why! If it isn't Sachidevi, Indra's pious wife and fellow

schemer!' Aja mimicked, even as every instinct urged her to flee. Or at least hold her tongue.

'Whores have no business addressing their betters nor do they belong in the sacred abode of Mahadeva,' Sachi said, a fanatical gleam in her eyes. 'Guards! Take this pox-addled wretch away from here before she pollutes this place with her foul presence.'

'You have no authority here,' Aja was surprised at how calm she sounded, though she knew with dead certainty that this was the bad end her mother had predicted for her, 'or anywhere in *my* brother's realm for that matter. It is my suggestion that you take yourself out of here before you make the trouble you clearly came here to.'

The guards who had moved towards her stopped in their tracks, glancing back at their mistress in mild confusion. Soora had sent the Devas into exile making the decision not to have them executed on account of the fact that they were his half-brothers. He wouldn't be so magnanimous if his sister's honour was impugned. As for Taraka...if he heard about this little fracas he would see it as adequate grounds to relieve them of flesh and bone, decreeing that it be fed to his hounds.

'Have a care how you address my mother!' the youth bellowed.

Aja ignored him. He was just a cub. All her attention was focused on his mother. This was the one she must face down. They were all bound to Sachi's will and acted as abominably cruel creatures, in concert with her commands. She was alone and cornered with nothing but her instincts to help her and they were telling her that the thread of her life had unspooled as far as it would go. *So be it, I am not one to prolong the inevitable by kicking and screaming. What will be, will be.*

'You are here to provoke a confrontation,' Aja spoke quietly. 'Indra is tired of waiting. With this ill-advised move to assault me, you seek to unleash the wrath of my brothers. Their sorrow and pain on my account will manifest in an avenging, killing fury that will pour over the three worlds like an unstoppable avalanche. Taraka will bathe Bhoomi Devi with the blood of every single one of the crores of Devas. He will not rest till your beloved Amaravati is sacked; till nothing remains of it but waste and burning ashes. Soora and Simha may not want to stop him. They may not even be able to.

'The immortals won't die quietly. They will release every one of the celestial *astras* capable of destroying entire worlds, taking many of my people and the mortals as well with them. You would have triggered mass murder on an unprecedented scale. All things good and bad, beautiful and ugly will be indiscriminately destroyed. The three worlds will be annihilated. Is that the price Indra and you are willing to pay to retake a crown and a throne?'

Aja felt something gather within her, uncoiling in a burst of moment, its power sweeping her along as it enveloped her senses. The words spilled forth from her lips seemingly of their own volition and she could actually see the smouldering remains of the three worlds reduced to waste and rubble. All too obvious was her part in all of this. This was where her meandering journey had led her. It was a terrifying thought.

There was horror in Sachi's eyes too as if she too could see it but it vanished in a heartbeat and Indra's consort too was propelled along the path she must take, led thither by a power that dwarfed them all.

Sachi glared at her in cold fury. 'How dare you? One of your ilk has no right to presume to know or even begin to comprehend the honourable actions of the righteous King of Heaven. You are a filthy whore and always have been one. Your conduct has been so reprehensible, your own mother cursed you and foretold that your end would be an infamous and ignominious one.'

Aja trembled ever so slightly, duly noting that being cognizant of one's part in the larger scheme of things engineered by fate and destiny did little to inure one from the pettiness of a small mind or mean spirit. The barb had drawn blood, Sachi noted with savage satisfaction.

Even her Lord, the Wielder of the Thunderbolt had acknowledged that she had an uncanny ability for singling out an adversary's weakest spot. 'I don't blame Maya at all. Clearly she is all too familiar with your predilection for perversion. In a former life, you were Chitrarekha, wedded to the virtuous ascetic, Pundarika. The holy man could not satisfy your insatiable desire, and so you were driven into the arms of many men, including the sage Durvasa. Two sons were born out of your shame—the monsters Ilvala and Vatapi, both truly their mother's sons. In addition to being cannibals who grew fat on the flesh of the living, they sought to appropriate the ascetic merit Durvasa had painstakingly accrued over the aeons and he cursed them...'

'I am familiar with the tale,' Aja tried to reply as nonchalantly as she could, hating the tremor in her voice. Ilvala and Vatapi had been consumed by sage Agastya and he had digested their remains. As for Chitrarekha, the wrath of Durvasa, who had never forgiven her for inciting his dormant lust, had pursued her and she had concealed herself in a herd of goats. The easily angered sage, known for his curses, had decreed that she take birth among the Asuras as a goat-faced princess and pay the price for her perfidy. Maya had told her all this in a fit of spite, she remembered, when she had been a child. Her father, Sage Kashyapa, had taken the memory from her, she recalled, so that she need not live with the implications.

It was all coming back in dizzying waves and she reeled on her feet. Sachi laughed then. The sound was explosive and it reminded her of bowels being noisily voided, of carrion birds ripping out chunks of flesh, of her mother's hateful words and deeds from a troubled past of which she could never be free even after death had taken her away.

Pain and rage, spawned over a lifetime of inflicted hurt, endless taunting and callous shaming, a veritable ocean of it which she had so carefully dammed deep in her subconscious, boiled over and surged to the surface. *If I am to pay the price for perfidy, then I may as well earn it!*

Aja, the Goat-faced One, launched herself on her antagonist. Or was it her mother she was seeing in her adversary's stead? Maya of the cruel taunts, who had not hesitated to sacrifice her children on the altar of boundless ambition… The look of surprise and naked terror in her victim's eyes made her feel more euphoric than she had ever felt in this lifetime. With brute force worthy of Tarakasura himself, she landed a few well-placed blows with the full power of her repressed rage, right on that pert mouth which was usually pursed in disapproval but which at that precise moment was hanging open in slack jawed shock. Artfully made up lips split like overripe plums and blood gushed out in a satisfying stream.

Fingernails raked across cheeks, gouging out ribbons of glacial facial tissue before closing in on the scrawny windpipe, taut with tension, anxious to snuff the life that stubbornly flickered in hate-filled eyes glaring out of the bloodied mess of a face. Calloused hands latched into various parts of Aja's body, like burly worms that dug into her flesh with relish, filling her with revulsion as they tried to pull her away from their mistress.

She resisted might and main, refusing to let go, even when they stuck their daggers into her. Even as the sharpened points plunged in and out, blood spraying in all directions, Aja tightened her grip and had almost succeeded in crushing the life out of Sachi, when the blow from a spiked club crashed into the base of her skull.

Aja couldn't be certain of the things that happened next. A killing blow to the head could do that, exacerbating the confusion that all life was mired in, kicking up a frenzied dust storm to obliterate from living memory the horrors that transpired in the blood-soaked passage of a soul from a rapidly dissolving present to the vastness of an unknown future.

Confronting the vast vistas that stretched ahead of her, beyond death filled her with exhilaration and she could practically feel her spirit sprouting wings. She had served the needs of one who carried within him the sacred flame. One she had loved with the entire force of her being without ever knowing that it was so. She had searched for him endlessly over the aeons and now she lay before him in abject surrender, to become one within him. Finally she was as complete as she wanted to be.

He was a force of nature that carried the sparks of life itself. It was his role, she realized, to shatter everything before gathering together the scattered bits, making them whole again and imbuing them with meaning. And he had chosen her to be a part of his grand design.

In light of her new-found awareness she realized that what preceded the conjoining was entirely irrelevant. Of absolutely no importance. Even the violating of a body that had been her own for an entire lifetime or the hacking of former hands, and the rest of it, orders being executed by an enemy's ego.

Her lack of interest went further. Somewhere at the periphery of a dwindling consciousness she could sense the triggering of a chain reaction that led to more of the violence and destruction that had marked the end of her existence, leading to the three worlds being awash in a crimson tide of blood. In large part on her account. Yet, none of it seemed to matter. Not even a little. Not even a lot.

From this vantage perspective, death was a mercy and a blessing, both. Knowing this there was no need for further remonstration or recrimination. It was time to go where her considerably lighter spirit led her. Towards bliss and salvation. Without looking back or lingering for one last look at a beloved Linga bathed in her lifeblood or the bloodbath that was to follow.

Blood For Blood

NEEDLESS TO SAY, there were repercussions to the brutal murder of Ajamukhi. For how were the living to know that the one they mourned had gone on to a better place and was truly at peace? When her brothers, famed for their penchant for pugnacity, laid eyes upon the desecrated remains of their beloved sister whose back had been abominably mutilated and hands hacked off, their fury knew no bounds.

Bitterly regretting the clemency he had shown his defeated half-brothers, Soora sent his soldiers to capture every single Deva they could get their hands on, determined to make them answer for the sins of their callow King. Taraka had sworn vengeance and the three worlds trembled in fear. When he had seen the remains of Aja, he had grown berserk and begun killing everybody in the vicinity while in the throes of his black rage. It had taken the combined strength of Soora and Simha to overpower him and bring him to his senses. Or as close to such a state as it was possible under the circumstances.

Simha tried to curtail the rage of his brothers, advocating a more measured but equally devastating response. 'Don't you see what is happening?' he pleaded with Soora. 'Indra has made his move with the express purpose of manipulating our feelings for Aja to unleash a storm of brutality that we already have an undeserved reputation for. If Taraka is allowed to go on a rampage, too many of our innocent subjects will pay the price while Indra and his consort Sachi, having started this, will end up having the last laugh. They would have anticipated the fallout from their despicable actions and would have retreated to a cosy hidey hole beyond our reach, no doubt disguised as the worms they are.'

He paused for a few minutes, sensing that his words were bouncing off his brother like water off a duck's back. Taraka, not surprisingly, was looking at him with revulsion, mercifully rendered speechless by the vehemence of his displeasure over Simha's words. The object of his ire, meanwhile, was growing frustrated and he wondered why even Soora, who ought to know better, was behaving as if he had suggested that they all bend over for a good buggering.

But Simha was determined to talk sense into them. 'As always, Indra has engineered a crisis and he will look to Vishnu hoping he will obligingly scour out the three worlds with our blood. Or perhaps this time it is Shiva's son who will arrive to do the dirty work. This is not what Aja would have wanted...'

'Aja would have wanted to live,' Taraka growled, his voice hoarse with hatred, 'not die a horrible death at the hand of Indra's whore...' He could not go on and his hands were clenched tight. Simha knew that Taraka could barely control the urge to pluck out his tongue and pummel him bloody.

'You cannot stop me from making every single one of

those bastards pay for their dastardly deeds. Don't you dare try!' Taraka thundered. 'They cannot hide from me forever. I will overturn the three worlds and burn every living thing in it to the ground if that is what it takes to find them. Then I will make Indra watch as I chop up his wretched wife and feed every last piece to him. That is only the beginning of what I have planned for him. All who come in my way or seek to obstruct my search by shielding that bastard will know the full extent of my fury. And that goes for the two of you as well.'

Having said all he wished to say on the matter and anxious to bloody his hands, Taraka stormed off. Simha made to follow. His brother's foolhardiness had stirred his own anger and he was determined to knock some sense into his head with his fists if need be. Soora stopped him with an imperious gesture.

'Every word you have uttered has merit, Simha, and I could not be prouder of you!' Soora's voice was calm. 'Even so, I urge you to let him go. Taraka only goes to do what he feels is a perfectly justified course of action. It is all any of us can do. Events have spiralled out of our control and it will be foolish on our part to pretend otherwise. Aja was the sister of a King and the best of us all. Hers was a blameless existence insofar as such a thing is possible and there must be consequences for those who rob the three worlds of the good people in it.'

'Not if it means robbing the same three worlds of even more good and innocent people! Not if we refuse to break this vicious cycle of endless hate!' Simha insisted. 'When driven by anger our actions are indiscriminate and always inexcusable. I too grieve for Aja but mass murder is certainly not going to bring her back. By our actions, all we will succeed in doing is excoriate her memory, for people will blame her when they become victims of Taraka's killing frenzy and curse her with their last breath. She will be remembered not for her beautiful spirit or her generous nature or as someone who spent her life actively avoiding violence but as a monster who was responsible for the madness that engulfed the three worlds, heralding the beginning of the end. If that were not unbearable enough we will be playing right into Indra's hands and he will laugh himself silly over the unspeakable tragedy that is unfolding all around us even as we waste time talking.'

'In this matter, Indra exercises as much control as we do which is next to nothing, despite the elaborate charades we play believing ourselves to be the holders of absolute power,' Soora told him in that same voice of quiet resignation and at that moment, Simha, the lionhearted, trembled ever so slightly as a frisson of terror clawed its way up his spine.

However, when his momentary weakness had faded, he focused on what his brother and King was telling him. 'There are forces at play here that we cannot begin to comprehend. All of us have been given roles in this farce and it behoves us to enact it to the best of our abilities. If that entails every one of your darkest fears being realized, then so be it!'

That is the end of that! Simha thought morosely to himself. They were going to their deaths. He knew that for certain now. But he hoped that there was something better than the sum of all their fears on the other side. For all their sakes. Shaking his head one last time, he bowed to the reigning monarch of the three worlds, acceding to his will.

The hunt for Indra and the rest of his absconding Devas began in earnest. Soora himself waylaid Surya as he was fleeing across the skies in his fiery chariot, killing his noble steeds and smashing his vehicle to smithereens. The Sun God was forcibly relieved of his golden diadem and shorn of his countless rays before being trussed up in chains and tossed into a dark dungeon. The three worlds became dank and dismal without his radiance but Soora was past caring.

Vayu and Varuna, Lords of the Wind and Sea joined hands to put up an almighty resistance. Violent gale winds and hurricanes pummelled the strongholds of the Asuras with vicious intent, hammering away at their resistance in relentless gusts tearing apart edifices of stone and iron as though they were made of reeds. Homes of the humble and rich were alike blown apart to bits before Maya's first born, possessed of an indomitable spirit and unmatched valour, fought his way past the bilious gusts and killing squalls to bring Vayu to his knees.

Varuna unleashed the tidal waves and his sea monsters, uncaring that too many humans would lose their lives in the almighty clash with their half-brothers. Monstrous walls of white water washed away everything in sight, flooding the plains and drowning pretty much every human being, bird and animal. The monsters dredged up from the merciless depths of the ocean floor and the water bodies over which Varuna presided attacked the enemies of their overlord, stalking the shoreline and spreading terror in all directions.

Enormous many-headed serpents coiled their bodies around hundreds, crushing them with their bulks or dragging them to a watery grave, spewing their poisons every which way. Giant krakens and squids reached out with grasping tentacles and suckers with jagged edges extending in all directions, latching on to hapless victims, impervious to their cries for mercy.

Nightmarish creatures of all shapes and sizes rose from the depths of darkness and shadow, their eyes slits of pure malevolence, features twisted with bestial passion, advancing in relentless waves, moving as one with savage precision, preying on all who fled before them in blind panic irrespective of whether they belonged to the race of Deva, Asura or man.

Simhamukha, fighting with peerless courage, ever dedicated to his belief that all life was precious, went above and beyond the call of duty to save as much of it as he could. Single-handedly, he took on the terrible creatures, his golden trident soaked in blood and slime as he chased the ones he hadn't skewered to death back into the cesspool that had spawned them.

His best efforts notwithstanding, Varuna was no match for the ferocity of Maya's son who withstood an army of rampaging octopodes and poison-spewing serpents, incinerating them with his fiery missiles. The Lord of the Waters had no choice but to surrender to his mercy even though he knew it would not be forthcoming if Taraka and Soora had their way. Certainly not after his decision to unleash the sea monsters.

The extent of the devastation wrought by the almighty clash between the Asuras and the Devas was beyond anything that could be conceived. Vast plains lay buried under the floods, dense forests lay in shambles, majestic trees lay uprooted and broken, bereft of life, crops that had been ready for the harvest were laid to waste. All around there were the bloated corpses of every form of life.

Chained and muzzled like a rabid dog, Vayu was thrown into a cage, one among the many kennels that provided accommodation for the rest of the King's hounds and bitches. It was so narrow, he was forced to crouch on all fours. Adding to the indignities heaped upon him, the Wind God was fed along with them, and actively encouraged to fight for bits of bone and meat at spear point. Varuna fared even worse for the antics of his pets. He was chained to a rock, his feet left hanging to roast over live coals, and fed the rotting innards of his own decomposing creatures.

Yama, Lord of the chthonic realms was left to fend off the rage of the evillest of evil creatures, whom he had personally condemned to his thousand hells. They had been granted an early release thanks to the large-heartedness of the Asura King. Reeling under the sheer weight of their numbers, he fought them off again and again using his fabled weapons, while his captors jeered, but no sooner had he succeeded in trapping them behind the barriers of hell than they were set free again, so that his personal experience of hell remained uninterrupted.

Without Yama to hold them back, the hordes of his thousand hells surged into the realms of the living, wreaking their especial brand of havoc on those who had little to fend them off with.

The Ashwini twins were forced to nurse the wounded Asuras and deny care to their own. Any protest, however mild, led to the infliction of grave injuries on their own persons which they were not allowed to treat. Agni languished in the sewers deep in the underbelly of Mahendrapuri dealing with the twin evils of being buried under foul smelling bodily waste and enormous rats that seemed intent on helping themselves to any chunks of his flesh they could gouge out with their sharp teeth. But lamentable as their fate was, these were the lucky ones.

Taraka refused to be mollified by what he viewed as merciful measures implemented against those who had done little to deserve it. He was determined to wage his own personal vendetta against the Devas and so commenced the slaughter and butchery in earnest. His informers brought in those convicted of complicity with the Devas, or the wretched souls accused of aiding and abetting them. They paid no mind to the fact that the majority of those apprehended had no inclination to get involved in the shenanigans of those in power, cursing Deva and Asura alike for jointly reducing the three worlds to rubble. Most were unfortunate wretches for whom things were about to get a whole lot worse.

On the orders of Taraka, his men cooked victims in boiling vats of oil, skewered prisoners and while they were still alive, roasted them on slowly rotating spits. Some were used for target practice. Others were fed to crocodiles, who were starved first so their appetite would be keener and their natural meanness increased a hundredfold. Many were impaled and left to rot to serve as a warning to those who failed to join the hunt for the Devas, who, it was believed, numbered thirty-three crores. Taraka was determined to capture them all and force them to give up Indra and Sachi, before executing his plan to exterminate his murderous half-brothers.

Soma, the Moon God's favourite wife was taken captive and he was assured that she would be subjected to cruel ill-usage if he failed to devise ingenious methods to torture his friend Kubera into revealing Indra's whereabouts. In the meantime, the latter's vast stores of treasure had been plundered and his followers, the fierce Yakshas, annihilated. Amaravati, the capital city of the Devas, was sacked and the Asuras set fire to the fine palaces and destroyed its famous gardens and priceless artefacts. Pyramids of skulls shot up all over the three realms, grotesque mountains that sprang up overnight as a testament to the folly of those who ought to know better.

When Jayanta was brought to him already more dead

than alive because he had insisted on resisting his captors, Taraka had the skin flayed off his back and tortured him for days, cutting off parts of his body until only the severed head remained. This was skewered on a spear and displayed from the ramparts.

Nobody knew what had become of Indra and Sachi, where they were, or if they were even alive. In the early days, it was believed that the couple were in the guise of parrots and the Lord of Thunder was biding his time and gathering an army for an attack. It was rumoured that the deposed monarch had taken the life of his wife to spare her from the wrath of Taraka before taking the extreme step himself. All hope seemed to have vanished with the missing couple and despair enshrouded the three worlds. And still the bloodshed went on, unabated.

A Sea of Voices

KARTIKEYA HEARD THE cries of the living, dead and dying all the time now. A horrible howling that would abate to incessant mewling as they raised their voices in unison begging him to intervene and release them all from their suffering. The voices had built to an ear-splitting crescendo, becoming increasingly intrusive, edged as it was with their white-hot anger and unbearable agony.

'Shanmugha! It was prophesized that you would deliver us from evil! What in heaven's name are you waiting for?'

'Skanda! While you are engaged in frivolous play on the heights of your father's abode, this accursed war rages on! Make it stop!'

'Deliver us from evil! How can you turn a deaf ear to our entreaties? How can you be so impervious to our suffering? Why won't you answer our prayers?'

'Your parents should have another child already, seeing that you will not come to our aid...'

'There is no God! And if there is, he or she is every bit as bad as those who oppress us! Curse you all!'

Not all of it was the angered exhortations born of misery. Many called out to him from a deep wellspring of love and simple faith. They were willing to brave all the suffering in the world if it meant drawing closer to him. With unwavering confidence, they waited. It seemed incredible, but their belief was unshakeable, even when they faced unceasing torment and died like flies.

Then there were the few who believed in nothing. Not even themselves, and certainly not in a divine entity who was supposedly born from another divine entity's hyper charged ejaculate to save them all. They fought when they could, endured as far as it was possible to and busied themselves with the arduous business of survival.

Not that death and misery spared any of them. Those too, like everything else—joy and sorrow, pain and pleasure, health and sickness, wealth and penury—bestowed their attentions on the deserving and the undeserving with a rigid adherence to their preferred code of impartial arbitrariness.

The child no longer roamed the heights of Mount Kailash in cheerful play and endless exploration of the halcyon experiences of extreme youth. Instead he had withdrawn deep into himself, going further and further into the wild, solitary spaces of his soul. He had given himself over entirely into silence and stillness. Lost in contemplation, he stared into the distance, waiting and watching.

Parvati watched Karti prepare for the arduous trial by fire that awaited him in silent admiration. He was so perfect and so brave! There would never be another to equal him. Even so, she wished she could spare him everything that lay ahead or at the very least, shoulder the burden for him.

'Talk to him!' she whispered to Shiva, who was driving her to distraction by being every bit as nonchalant as she was agitated. Parvati would have gone to him but her emotions were all over the place and she had half a mind to summon the Shaktis that raged within her and unleash them, putting an end to the endless conflict that had been raging since the beginning of time for which there would never ever be a cessation. Aware that his wife was dangerously close to losing her temper with him, the three-eyed God obliged, even though he personally felt that Karti was doing just fine by himself.

Sneaking up on his son, Shiva lifted him up and placed him firmly on his lap. As always he was taken aback by the force of feeling, the rush of affection he felt for his son. 'I am too grown up for this sort of thing,' Karti groused to mask his pleasure at being on the receiving end of his father's undivided attention. Sometimes he was quite contrary, just like his mother. Besides if he hated it so much he could have easily wriggled out of his grasp, the way he was sometimes wont to, when he felt the need to reiterate his status as a grown-up.

'Your mother certainly doesn't think so! As far as she is concerned, you will always be a baby to be cuddled and cooed over!' Shiva teased him. With a pang, he realized that by dealing with the imbroglio involving the Asura brothers, Karti would indeed undergo a transformation.

'What is bothering you, son?' he asked, holding the warm body close to his chest. 'Is it the voices in your head again?'

'Do you hear them too?' Karti wanted to know.

Shiva nodded in assent. 'Your mother hears them too. As does your uncle Vishnu. Sometimes it gets to be a little much, doesn't it?'

'What do you do when it does?' he absent-mindedly tugged on the tail of the serpent that reposed on his neck.

'For a brief moment, I am tempted to open my third eye and turn the three worlds to a smouldering pile of ashes just to quell the endless clamouring...' Shiva said, only half in jest, 'but the urge passes and I realize that the voices, every single one of them, are my own.'

'Exactly!' Karti leaned against his father's chest in relief. 'I sensed that when things feel this awful, you had to be the root cause of it. Mother would most certainly agree.' He laughed at his own joke before picking up the hopelessly tangled skein of his thoughts again. 'If the voices are yours, then they begin and end with you. As for me, since I too have emerged from you, I will return to you, no matter where I choose to go. All that remains for me to do is still the chaos in my head and all will be tranquil within. But that, of course, is easier said than done.'

'That is true. None of it is easy. Not for me nor your mother. And it applies to everybody as well. But awareness is the beginning. It is the precise moment when truth takes root. Nothing happens overnight. Not even when willed by the Gods. And yet, when the seed of enlightenment achieves full maturity it would seem to have happened in a heartbeat. The way forward will be known to you and illuminated by the knowledge you have gained.'

Karti nodded vigorously, his soft curls bouncing against his father's strong shoulders. Shiva sensed the lad's terrible loneliness even as he was with his parents and an army of their devotees. How could he not? The boy's solitude was his own. As was the fiercely independent streak. His wild and untameable spirit came from his mother though. The remarkable good looks he got from both of them as well as the verve and vigour.

Quietly, he spoke again, 'The important thing to remember is that though the journey you are to undertake must be your own, you are not alone. All things in existence are connected to all else and the threads that bind us together may be gossamer—soft and delicate, but they are strong enough to withstand being torn apart despite being pulled in all directions by the best efforts of every single thing they hold together. Is that not remarkable?'

'It *is* remarkable,' his son agreed. 'It makes it all worthwhile, I suppose. Besides, if my best efforts amount to nought, you can always follow through on your threat to open your third eye and burn it all to cinders!'

This time Shiva laughed too. Seeing her boys in such good spirits, Parvati smiled and it widened when Vishnu, the Divine Preserver and her own Lord's dearest friend arrived borne aloft on Garuda, the mighty Eagle who was the King of all winged creatures, and was supposedly so strong, he could bear the weight of Bhoomi Devi and all her creatures on a single feather. Their coming was a good sign, Parvati knew.

Karti was fond of Vishnu too and his great winged mount and he ran to greet their guests, exuberance lighting up his features. 'Where is your *chakra*?' he asked without preamble. 'I knew your index finger would grow fatigued from holding it up aloft all the while even as it spins round and round in never-ending circles.'

'You know the answer to your own question...' Vishnu wagged his finger at him.

'Of course I do,' Karti chirped. 'When Tarakasura landed at Vaikunta, you submitted to the will of fate and allowed Maya's son to prevail. But not before hurling your *chakra* at him to stop him from laying waste to your abode. He is now forced to wear it around his neck where it continues to spin uninterrupted in that dizzying fashion. Some say that was the precise moment when he went from being an evil villain to becoming the evillest of villains.'

'Precisely! It has been decreed that only Shiva's son can stop the ravages wrought on the three worlds by the *karma* of Maya's sons. Many among the mortals and immortals have begged me to urge you to act and I have come on their behalf,' Vishnu told him with a smile, before turning to address his parents. His movements were unhurried, and for someone who had been sent to apprise him of a dire situation and urge haste, he behaved as though they had all the time in the world.

Vishnu and Shiva embraced like brothers. The Protector then greeted Parvati with a smile and presented her with a bouquet of wild flowers he had gathered from the same spot where she had performed intense *tapas* to win her beloved, knowing that they were her favourites. His thoughtfulness touched her deeply, and she breathed in their fragrant perfume which, for her, would always be the scent of the first flush of love.

'They are beautiful! This is so nice of you!' she enthused and then added more hesitantly, 'I am sorry to have cursed that your consort will remain barren. It is known to me that you did your best to dissuade the Devas from intruding on Shiva and me.'

'There is no need for you to apologize. When issued from your lips even a curse is a blessing and I am grateful!' The sincerity in his words was unmistakeable and Parvati was grateful. With a mischievous glance at Karti, he added, 'Besides everybody knows that children are so pleasing to look upon simply to dissuade parents from flinging them off a cliff when they get to be too much trouble!'

With those words, he lifted Karti in his hands, pretending to fling him as far as he could and them spun him around in circles, lowering him to the ground only when he was sure the lad wouldn't be able to walk straight.

'He is too grown-up for that sort of thing!' Shiva guffawed and the foremost of the Gods burst into raucous laughter together. If only the mortals and the rest of the immortals could see this scene! They would be convinced that their worst fears had been realized and the Gods were truly indifferent to their plight, given how they were indulging in outright tomfoolery.

And yet, this was the precise moment when hope had been resurrected. The war would be over soon and a new order would emerge from the ashes of the old. The sun would rise on a new, golden age and for a while at least, all would be bright and beautiful again.

'I come bearing presents,' Vishnu told Karti who seemed to have cheered up considerably. Garuda, who had been watching the proceedings in silence stepped forward and placed the offerings of the Devas in front of Shiva's son who examined the splendid treasures on display with mild curiosity. There was gold aplenty, and silver, in addition to crowns, diadems, a whole lot of jangly jewellery and great mounds of precious stones.

Even more impressive were the weapons they had sent, no doubt an oblique hint to get off his behind, pick them up and charge into war. There was a heavy golden trident, an ancient war bow with inexhaustible quivers, swords with exquisite markings and ornate hilts, wicked looking clubs, maces, spears, and lances, bejewelled daggers, a helmet with dazzling workmanship, an impenetrable suit of armour, a gilded chariot, fine garments and thousands of other accoutrements that could outfit an entire army.

There were flowers, fruits, fine cuts of meat, jars of the nectar of immortality, vintage wines and sweetmeats aplenty, probably intended to sweeten his disposition and make him more expansive in the hope that Shiva's son would harken to their plea. Having studied the many gifts that had been sent, Karti set them aside and stood up.

'I thank you for these blessings and the affirmation of faith in me but I am afraid that there I have no use for any of these implements.' His words were gracious but firm. 'The gifts given to me by my father and mother on the occasion of my birth are more than sufficient for the task at hand.' No sooner had he said these words, the dazzling display disappeared. Shiva beamed with pride.

Garuda stepped forward hesitantly and Karti turned to him with a smile. 'You come bearing a gift too. The one I have been waiting for! Let me see him! Don't worry, I will not make this one vanish too.'

The great bird smiled, and said, 'I should hope not, for my gift to you is a beloved son. His name is Chitrabahn and he is my wife Unnati's favourite. This youngster is our pride and joy, and like me, he is a devourer of snakes, seeking only to serve by the side of one who is worthy. And there is none in the three worlds who is worthier than you!'

Kartikeya's eyes lit up when they alighted on the most dazzling creature in all of creation. The graceful bird was a scintillating shade of blue, chased with iridescent hues of green, gold and bronze. His neatly crafted head stood atop a slender, graceful neck with a tuft that was grander than the most richly wrought crowns or diadems. An exquisite train fanned out over his sturdy tail in a blaze of riotous colour—yellow, green and blue flowing into a bright violet, a marvellous blend over which a hundred eyes flashed at him, more brilliant than the sparkling gems that had been displayed before him in a glittering array, mere moments ago.

The peacock's bearing was majestic and full of dignity. The sunbeams bathed this sublime being with light to better drink in his beauty, and his eyes shone with intelligence. Kartikeya was speechless and when Chitrabahn addressed him with a truly distinctive voice that to the untrained ear sounded awfully close to discordant shrieking, he could not have been more delighted. He placed his hand on the bird's arched neck and stroked him. This gesture prompted his new mount to cleave to Kartikeya's side, slipping effortlessly into his chosen role. Forever more, he would be the bosom companion of Karti, Shiva's son.

Garuda's eyes were wet with tears. 'In a former age, I got into an argument with one of Shiva's Bhutaganas who claimed that his Lord was greater than mine. It shames me to say that our argument got out of control. More and more joined in, taking sides, resulting in vitriolic disagreement, heated arguments and intolerance, which in turn led to a bout of fisticuffs. Our discord spilled over to the rest of the three worlds and much blood was shed as the followers of Vishnu and Shiva turned on each other, though the great Gods in question have only ever loved and respected each other.

'To make amends for our misguided actions which had such fell consequences, we swore a blood oath to work together to curb similar madness and contribute to the greater glory of Shiva and Vishnu both. Which is why in this age, I have the privilege of fathering the Bhutagana, a great favourite of the three-eyed God, who has taken several births to earn the honour of serving as your vehicle.'

'You have my gratitude,' Kartikeya was serious, 'for this gift is precious and I will treasure it for all of eternity. The time had come for me to leave with my new friend. I have tarried here long enough.'

He seems to be in a great hurry to leave, and is ever so eager even! Parvati noted, her heart growing heavy with grief at their imminent parting. Nothing would be the same again. She watched him hug his father and uncle Vishnu goodbye. To her irritation, Shiva seemed to be handling this very well. He murmured a few encouraging words and even cracked a joke or two which made their son smile.

When it was her turn, she blessed the boy putting her heart and soul into it, willing every ounce of the love she bore to him to shield him from the malevolent forces that already dogged him. Too overcome to speak, she kissed the top of his head and bid him farewell.

Without further ado, he climbed atop his peacock and the bird spread its gorgeous feathers, soaring heavenwards. In mid-flight they turned around abruptly. Karti leaped off and rushed back to his mother who gathered him in a fierce embrace. 'How like your father you are! And I do not mean that as praise! Ride to glory my son and remember, even when you leave me and we are separated by time and space, I will still be with you, every step of the way!'

'And so will I, Mother! That is a promise.'

Parvati watched as her boy flew from the nest which he had blessed with his presence. She watched till he became a tiny speck and long after he disappeared into the distance.

The Girl in the Golden Cage

'WHERE ARE WE going?' Chitra wanted to know. 'Will you gather together a rebel army to lead a charge against Soora? Will the Ganas and your mother's Shaktis supplement the ranks of those who follow you into battle? Will there be an almighty conflict marked by the unloosing of celestial missiles that will level the three worlds before Soora, Simha and Taraka are ground into the dust never to bother anybody again?'

'So many questions! Mercifully the answer to all of them is the same—I haven't the faintest notion,' Karti replied. He was enjoying the ride immensely. His lovely mount was a great one for talking and it wasn't entirely a bad thing, given that the curiously hoarse cries when amplified by the wind took on the thundering tones of a furious storm or an angry ocean scaring away friend and foe alike. In fact, the strident notes of his unmelodious tones quietened even the voices in his head.

'Your followers who wait in the hopes that you will swoop in on your exquisite *vahana* and rescue them all are going to be so thrilled!' Chitra chittered on, while Karti wished he would expend his energy towards achieving the soaring heights his father did, instead of squawking and hovering as close to the treetops as he dared without inviting the accusation of cowardice. 'But how are they to know that you are not dithering but merely teaching them an invaluable lesson on the futility of waiting for heroes to come to the rescue when they should be expending all their strength and energy on making better lives for themselves?'

He was still chattering nineteen to the dozen about the complicated workings of the universe and how frustrating it was to make the attempt to unravel its mysteries when they chanced upon her. Or at least Karti did. 'Do you see the girl, Chitra? Speaking of the complicated workings of the universe, isn't it funny that we somehow managed to stumble on this one in the middle of nowhere?'

'I don't see anything!' he replied. 'It is said that there is a nameless Goddess of War, who is most beauteous to look upon and she entices warlike males to follow her into battle with extravagant promises of blood, gold and other pleasures. Perhaps it is her…'

Karti scoffed, 'My mother told me that is yet another ridiculous tale made up by those who seek to blame the female of every species for all the lamentable occurrences in the three worlds. Besides, this one will not be leading anyone anywhere soon. She seems to be trapped in a cage.'

However, she *was* beautiful. Her skin was the colour of rich cream and he could tell that it would be soft to touch. There was a gentleness and serenity to her that he found most appealing. Eyes that were huge, dark and luminous were fastened on him and there was a certain spark and intriguing depth to them which drew him to her most powerfully. Despite her unfortunate predicament, she seemed unruffled, intently engaged with combing out the tangles in her hair, by running her fingers through them patiently and plaiting the thick coils as though she somehow knew that he was on his way to her.

Chitra was already attuned to the nuances of his master's thought processes and as they landed, he remarked, 'Maya's sons have waited a long time for your attention and I suppose waiting just a little bit longer while you linger over the promise of romance can't hurt them.' There was only the mildest hint of irony in his tone. 'I see her now! It is to be wondered what act of witchcraft led to her being thus imprisoned.'

Ordinarily, Karti would have commented on his suspicious bent of mind but he was too enthralled by the maiden. Sensing his approach, the mysterious girl turned, a welcoming smile spreading across her stunning features. Excitedly, she gripped the bars of her cage with a sudden display of strength, tightening her hold and urgently gesturing for him to do the same.

When Kartikeya's hands closed over hers, the solid gold bars snapped as though they were made of twigs as even the elements thrilled to the magnetic force that flowed between them and swirled in a joyous flow on the conjoining of kindred spirits who were made for each other. He helped her out of the cage, and she smiled up at him. 'I knew you would come!'

'Stranger and stranger! My father is fond of saying that you find love in the unlikeliest of places. He himself found my mother, Unnati, the parrot, on the ashes of her master Kamadeva when your father, in his endless wisdom, saw fit to reduce him to such a lamentable state,' Chitra rasped and the spell was broken.

'What an extraordinarily exquisite bird!' she cooed in a dulcet tone that was achingly familiar, for he had heard it in his dreams often, 'but what an unfortunate voice it has!'

'Careful there!' Karti laughed. 'He is sensitive! Why don't you tell me who you are and how you came to be put in a cage?'

'This should be interesting...' Chitra commented. Karti ignored him.

'My name is Devasena,' the girl began, 'this cage belongs to Dharma and I have been here for a long time now, waiting for you.'

'The girl is bait!' Chitra exclaimed, his voice pitched at an excruciatingly high level. 'Devasena is derived from Devendra, one of Indra's many names. He must have left her here in this enchanted cage, hoping to draw out Tarakasura who is hot for revenge and would like nothing better than to get his hands on this sweet child here and relieve her of hands as well as honour and life to repay Indra and Sachi for what they did to his sister Ajamukhi. The Wielder of the Thunderbolt grows desperate and is willing to dirty his hands and sully his conscience in order to induce you to intervene.'

Devasena stared at him in bewilderment, heroically resisting the urge to shut her ears.

'He is saying that you must be the most obedient daughter, if you are willing to remain in a cage in furtherance of your father's grandiose plans. Especially since these are hostile times where those with less than honourable intentions towards your person are looking high and low for you and your family members,' Karti said.

'I will have no part in my father's designs or his wars,' the girl said raising an elegant eyebrow in magnificent disdain. 'He wanted my brother Jayanta and me to accompany our mother when she went after poor Ajamukhi in the hopes of setting off a cataclysmic conflict. His heir is too precious so he planned to leave me behind to be taken hostage by Taraka. He said I was beautiful enough to entice you into saving me from the Asura; moreover, we are meant to marry and he felt that you would not allow your bride-to-be to come to grief.'

She said it very nonchalantly but her cheeks flushed and turned a delicate shade of crimson. Quickly, she resumed speaking. 'When I refused to be a part of his scheme, he accused me of being an ingrate and left me here to the mercy of whichever one of you stumbled upon me first.'

'I am sorry that you have been through such a terrible ordeal,' Karti told her.

Devasena smiled at him. 'Don't feel too sorry for me, there are so many out there who are going through so much worse. And I hope you won't think too badly of my father either. In his own way, he too is principled and only does what he genuinely believes to be the right thing.' *Besides I knew you would find me. We are meant for each other. Knowing this, even a cramped cage becomes a comfortable dwelling for a heart that beats in unison with yours.* She did not say the words out loud but he heard them anyway.

'It is good for you that she is willing to forgive her father for his atrocious conduct. The fact that you are even more beautiful than the two of us put together probably has nothing to do with it. Be that as it may, her mercy and compassion bodes well for you, since you have always been meant for another as well,' Chitra quipped. 'Some Goddess of War! Rather than leading you to a battlefield, our little romantic seeks to lead you into the quagmire of love, which is even worse, in my humble opinion.'

'I am not quite sure what he is going on about but if I sang as badly as your bird, I would keep my beak closed.'

Karti laughed, pleased to note that shocked indignation had rendered Chitra momentarily speechless.

'Don't worry about him. For the most part, he means well,' Karti assured her. 'Now tell me, how may I help you? If it is my protection you seek…'

'If my father has taught me anything at all, it is to rely on nobody to protect me; but thanks for the offer. For what it is worth, I wish to offer my services and do my part to help end this war. By your side.' Her tone was soft and she exuded so such warmth that he could not resist her even if he had been inclined to try.

'I am sure she will be a great help when you ride into battle. Those slender arms are more suited to wielding a needle than a weapon. Women have no place on a battlefield, unless, of course, they happen to be Durga or Kali.' Chitra was irrepressible and Karti could have sworn that he was jealous of a beauty that surpassed his own. But he did have a point.

'The battlefield may not be the safest place for you… Your very presence is likely to goad Taraka into further depths of infamy and viciousness,' Karti told her gently, testing her resolve.

Devasena did not disappoint. 'With you by my side, I would be a fool to worry over my safety. I cannot swing a sword or wield a bow, nor do I wish to, for mastering the science of weaponry is the surest way to devote a perfectly good existence to endless violence. There will be plenty of killing before this thing runs its course and I will not have a part in all of that. But now that you are here, Tarakasura no longer scares me and it is my intention to help my father. For I made a promise and it behoves me to keep it.'

'She means that now that she has revealed herself, Taraka and his minions will be here in a heartbeat,' Chitra muttered. 'The best way to help a wounded animal is to put it down. And since she abhors getting her hair mussed by indulging in violent activities, she will stay out of the way while you make mincemeat out of him. Our Devasena is a clever girl. Someday, she is going to make you a good wife, even though your mother is going to be far from happy about this burgeoning bond of love.'

Karti hushed Chitra before addressing Indra's daughter courteously, 'If that is what you wish, then far be it for me to dissuade you. Besides he will be here soon.' Gently, he took her hands in his and pointed in the direction from which Tarakasura, the scourge of the three worlds, would approach them.

The deep lush forest in which they had met gave way to a deep valley flanked by a massive mountains on other sides. They stood on a narrow outcrop overlooking the rocky stretch below with the jagged fissures that gave the impression of monstrous fangs bared in a snarl, hungry for blood. It was here that they would meet the hordes of Taraka. It shimmered in the heat, barren and vast, devoid of the slightest hint of life.

Devasena spoke again, while waiting for what they knew was coming, 'Taraka's enmity with my father goes back a long way. In another age, the Danava Vajranga was a force to be reckoned with. Not only was he brave and strong but renowned for his good heart and kindness. His subjects and many others, including some among the Devas, felt he was better suited to rule over the three worlds. But he did not covet power and retired deep into the wilderness with his pregnant wife,

Vajrangi. Father tracked him down.

'It pains me to go into particulars but Vajrangi was harassed, tortured, and repeatedly violated. In the end, she and her child did not survive. Vajranga did and he devoted all the life that was left to him in the performance of the severest of penances to seek retribution against the one who had wronged him so grievously. Taraka is the fruit of his penances.'

Her eyes were filled with tears and were dark with horror. 'During the sack of Amaravati, many were the Devas who fell defending our homes. Others had no choice but to flee because they knew Taraka would show them no mercy. They were right. He emasculated the ones he had captured, doing the bloody work himself like a monstrous butcher who revelled in the blood of his enemies. But that was not the worst of it all. He rounded up the children and the wives of the Devas, some among them pregnant. These were the ones who had not managed to flee, or been given the merciful release of death by their husbands and fathers who could not bring themselves to. They were stripped naked, forced to circumambulate the city and...' She could barely go on. 'Not a single one of the ladies or their children were spared. Parvati's curse was fulfilled.'

'Taraka has a lot to answer for. But one way or the other it will all be over soon,' Karti comforted her. 'This age draws to a close and when dawn breaks on the next one, there will be a redistribution of power, leading to fresh hope and the promise of a better world. Love and wisdom may just prevail over hatred and ignorance.'

'Yes, it will be over for my father and Taraka soon enough. But I really hope neither of them have to suffer any more than they already have. There has too much of that going around as it is.'

'Isn't that sweet?' Chitra couldn't resist saying. 'She wants what all girls want. A happy ending where everything is perfect as you please. I hope I am not around when she realizes that these things never last.'

'You will have your happy ending,' Karti addressed the lovely Princess. 'It will not last long, but while it does, it will be even better than perfect.'

'That is more than enough for me.' When she smiled for that moment at least, their dismal surroundings were bathed in the glow of its cheerful brightness.

There Will Be More Blood

$\mathcal{I}$T BEGAN AS a dull thrum from far off, seeming to fade away before it grew louder and louder, till their ears throbbed with its malicious vehemence. It was the sound of an advancing enemy army roiling towards them, an implacable maelstrom of hostility that quickened the pulse and chilled the blood. They could see the advancing dust cloud, flashes of metal from unsheathed weapons, outlines of chariots manned by armoured warriors moving so fast they seemed to be devouring the distance and advancing at the speed of a vicious tornado.

As they drew closer on the forbidding landscape of the undulating plain that stretched ahead of them, they could make out the features of the enemy soldiers as well as the colour of their flags and banners, even the sheen of perspiration that coated broad foreheads scrunched up in anticipation of the cataclysmic confrontation that was to follow. Chitra watched the Deva Princess surreptitiously but to her credit she did not flinch. However, she did draw closer to Kartikeya who placed an arm protectively around her.

At the dead centre, they could make out Tarakasura's chariot. His massive steeds had been set a killing pace, and they tore up the ground with mighty hooves, breathing fire from their nostrils. His massive helmet of bronze and gold leaf hugged his skull, exposing only his close-set eyes beneath fierce, bristling eyebrows. His full beard was lathered with sweat and some of it had dried to white salt.

Like a trickle at first, but gathering momentum, the straggling remains of the Devas, many from amongst the humans, and Shiva's warriors led by Nandi had materialized seemingly from thin air, beneath the bluff on which the trio stood. The more predatory of the birds and beasts joined them. Even so, the rebels were heavily outnumbered.

Kartikeya rode out on his mount to greet them and they gathered around, touching his outstretched hand. They seemed upbeat even as the enemy, numerous as the grains of sand and seeming to stretch out to infinity, advanced in a moving mass of vehicles and a solid wall of bronze. At a hundred paces, Taraka gave the signal to halt. His lips parted in a horrible simulacrum of a smile to reveal crooked teeth stained brown.

Chitra wondered if they were simply the result of a complete lack of oral hygiene or the more ominous explanation that he dined on his enemies, drinking their blood and gnawing on his bones. He wondered why he wasn't more scared. All that stood between them all and complete annihilation was Kartikeya—who had nursed at his mother's breasts mere days ago and had known nothing beyond her hugs and kisses. The closest he had come to war like activity was a bit of roughhousing with his father and his Bhootaganas.

Yet, there was something about him and those twinkling

eyes which held out the promise of mischief and *moksha* both that inspired supreme confidence that while he was near, there was absolutely nothing to fear. It wasn't only him. Devasena, who was herself little more than a girl stood next to Kartikeya at complete ease even as Tarakasura charged towards her spurred on by his venomous hatred. In fact, every single one of them who stood with Shiva's son seemed remarkably assured, even happy, as they waited for the embrace of certain death. The whole thing was ludicrous.

'I have no quarrel with Shiva's son,' Taraka's bull-like voice boomed across the battlefield. 'Hand over the murderous brute's daughter to me like a good boy and be gone! Don't get yourself killed over the likes of Indra and his toxic offspring.'

'It is known that Tarakasura is the mightiest warrior the three worlds has ever seen,' Kartikeya spoke in a childish treble, high and sweet. 'Even Vishnu, mounted on Garuda, had to submit to you and your superior might. The Sudharshana *chakra* spinning around your neck bears testament to your stupendous achievement. And yet the one who stands before me seeks not to fight his equals or superiors but has stooped to despicable depths of infamy and has been accused of slaughtering women, babies, the old and infirm. Who is guilty of murdering Indra's valiant if vainglorious son, and seeks to slay a daughter, both of whom are innocent of their father's crimes. How then can I stand aside and allow an elephant in rut who is a danger not only to others, but to himself as well, to proceed as he pleases?'

'But you did stand aside when Indra, the thrice-cursed mass murderer slew my sister, the blameless Ajamukhi!' Taraka raged and the grief he was stricken with was a terrible thing to behold. 'She too was innocent but you were not hot for her like you are for this one. Your seemingly altruistic attitude stems from your desire to wed and bed her. Shiva's son indeed! I name you unworthy and if you insist on obstructing my path, I will smash your paltry forces and make you watch as I tear your prettyling from limb to limb with my bare hands! Then it will be your turn to die.'

Sibilant voices hissed angrily behind Kartikeya at the insult. Even Chitra bristled with ill-conceived fury when the threat to his master and Devasena was issued. But Shiva's son was calm and unruffled. He turned and smiled reassuringly at the Princess who responded in kind.

The sight infuriated Taraka. It galled him that the wheel of time had not ground to a halt after the death of Aja. Everybody including himself woke up, ate, drank, made merry, pissed and shat just as before. Some like the offensive duo before him were lucky enough to lead a life that was bright, beautiful and flavoured with love. It galled him that no woman had ever looked at him the way the murderer's spawn looked at Kartikeya. He was used to gazes filled with ill-concealed dislike and revulsion, not adoration.

How was any of it fair? Raising his sword high in the air, he gave the signal to attack. It was about time Shiva's precious progeny realized what it meant to have loved and lost.

Responding to his command, his men took up the battle cry and launched a savage offensive. In the span of a heartbeat, the two massive armies locked horns together becoming a single, monstrous organism that writhed and heaved with the effort of killing. Arrows buzzed through the air, like angry bees striking their targets with a meaty thump. The volleys decimated thousands on both sides.

All around were the sounds of battle. There was the blaring

of conches and horns, the pounding of war drums and the song of ringing metal as lances and javelins tore through the air and into their victims. Grunting with pain the feral dogs of war surged over each other. Their senses were on high alert, and they heard amplified the clangour of weapons, clamour of battle, gushing of spilled blood and painfully drawn last breaths. They could actually taste death behind their tongues, foul as rotting fish and see the souls forcibly wrenched from bodies mangled beyond recognition as they hastened down the dark passage all must take. In their cases, sooner rather than later.

In the shimmering haze of heated fighting there was nothing to see but the detritus of war—puddles of blood, severed limbs, overturned vehicles, shattered wheels, the wounded, dead and dying. The entire vale overflowed with crimson blood and bloated corpses floated on the surface. But still the struggle raged on across the length and breadth of the valley, as the soldiers, stabbed, thrust and killed or got killed.

Taraka singled out the provoking figure of the girl who stood above him, proud and lovely, pity writ large on those wondrous eyes. It drove him to insanity and he made straight for her, hacking his way past those who dared throw themselves in his path and stepping on their corpses, bloodied to the elbows, he proceeded unhindered. Then Shiva's son stood before him, barring his path with his slight frame, mounted on a preening peacock of all things!

'Come little Lordling! My blade will have its fill of you before feasting on Indra's little princess.' He hurled his javelin as he taunted the lad. His aim was true. It flew hard and fast towards his intended victim's unprotected chest. Taraka's grin was ferocious as he anticipated the moment of impact, which would not so much stop the heart of Shiva's son but pierce it and leave it in itty-bitty pieces. He blinked as the javelin spun away at the last possible moment, clattering harmlessly as it fell by his feet.

His soldiers were filled with superstitious dread but seeing the boy exposed they were galvanized into action and they unloosed their spears as one, hurling it at him in a thunderstorm of steel. They watched with macabre fascination, willing their missiles to impale him every which way and leave his perfect body riddled with holes. It was their last thought as the sharpened point of their chosen weapon tore through their own hearts and pinned them down upon the stony floor.

Turning his attention to the girl, Taraka aimed a missile at her. The fighting came to a standstill as the force of its power hurtled into the wall of ancient stone instead. Deep fissures and cracks appeared in the rock face and with a roar, entire chunks of stone were ripped apart before hurtling into the teeming mass of soldiers below.

Impossibly, the boy and girl were unhurt. They cut fine, if incongruent, figures indeed—slim and graceful, bright of countenance with identical pretty curls that bounced in the breeze from the gale storm of fighting at their feet. Taraka, on the other hand, was begrimed and sore, his senses befuddled as his terrible, infallible weapons that should have killed the odious pair many times over had been turned aside leaving them none the worse for wear. How could it be?

His sorcery will not protect him and it will be all the more satisfying when I batter that beautiful face to bloody pulp, tear his chest open and pluck out his heart! Taraka closed the distance between them and came at Kartikeya in a headlong rush, brandishing his great war mace of such surpassing weight that he alone could lift it. The great weapon had a fearsome reputation, for it had smashed mountains, impenetrable fortresses and bashed in more heads than could be counted.

Given his bulk, Taraka moved with surprising rapidity, swinging his mace in wide arcs, bringing it down with crushing blows that would have reduced a dozen bull elephants to bloody pulp. In a contest of this nature, none in the three worlds could withstand the brute power of Tarakasura. And yet somehow a mere slip of a youth held firm, repelling his attack with nothing more than a smile.

Taraka struck the side of the boy's head and felt the power of that killing blow. Only it rebounded on him and he felt his strength which had always been an implacable force of nature crumble with the impact of that terrible blow. The boy stood before him, whole and unharmed watching with a strange light in his eyes that drove his adversary into a frenzy.

Casting aside the mace, he grabbed his sword, thrusting and parrying with brute force surrounding Shiva's son in a ring of bronze, determined to cut him to pieces and personally deliver the pickled remains to the Destroyer. In a series of lightning fast strikes, he grazed the side of his neck beneath a shapely ear, sliced open his chest, scored him along the ribs and thrust deeply into the flank. Taraka took a step back to examine his handiwork. Incredibly, the lad was unmarked.

Pain exploded in his head and radiated across the length and breadth of his body with malignant intent and he screamed aloud as blood fountained out in thick geysers from wounds to the neck, chest, and flank. He could see his ribs, stark and white where the blade had sliced the skin to the bone. Taraka screamed in horror. Something evil was happening to him.

The boy stood unmoving in front of him, his skin luminescent, smooth and unblemished, every curl in place as he patted his peacock and went on watching him with a compelling intensity that seemed to strip Taraka of his defences, leaving him naked and exposed, drawing him close till his eyes were blinded by the overpowering light which was anathema for one who was a creature of darkness and shadow.

Taraka felt the final dregs of his vast strength ebb away, though in the past, his prodigious stamina had never ever given out and he could have gone on for days without missing a beat. Yet, as the blood seeped out of him from the mortal wounds he himself had inflicted, he was weak as an infant. If Shiva's son were to attack now, he was powerless to counter a killing thrust from the *vel* which he held in his right hand.

What was Kartikeya waiting for? The boy had stayed his hand and wouldn't raise a finger against him. Taraka sank to his knees. The blood continued to seep out of him in a copious outpouring and he spat out the stuff that bubbled over in his mouth. Dying was not as bad as he had expected. In fact, Taraka had not felt this good, so curiously buoyant in ages. He could no longer hear the sounds of battle which seemed to have faded away into the distance. *It will all be over soon. I can rest…*

Taraka realized he did not mind any of it. Not anymore. It was nice to feel as good as he suddenly did when he looked into that beautiful countenance and saw a version of himself he hadn't even known was there. Perhaps this was a form of bewitchment. Quickly, he stole a glance at the battlefield, expecting to see a slaughterhouse. To his bewilderment, there was nothing to be seen save a sea of emptiness without a thing to hold onto.

Perhaps the blow to his head from his own hand had addled his brains. He had no wish to live on as a doddering, drooling imbecile. Maya's son, possessed with the strength of a thousand elephants, barred his chest and waited for the *vel* to pierce his chest. To end it all. And still Kartikeya waited.

Then the girl, Indra's daughter, the one he had so badly wanted to kill, stood before him. There was pity in her eyes. The same pity that had goaded him to madness on the eve of battle. But there was something else there as well. Taraka waited for the ravening anger, the all-encompassing rage that had sustained him all through his existence to break free and explode over the girl, the boy and the peacock.

To his surprise, he could no longer feel its corrosive burn inside him. He wasn't even hurting anymore. With every breath he took, he felt his strength return. Taraka looked at them both in wonderment and more than a little confusion.

'What is happening here?' he questioned the boy. 'I am not afraid of death. In fact, I have long been prepared for and even welcomed an unusually violent climax to this sordid existence of mine. It is nothing more or less than what I deserve. Why have you spared me?'

Kartikeya smiled, 'It is not what you deserve. Your death and destruction was never part of the plan. Especially when there is so much more that you have to offer.'

The voice and words were so comforting. They reminded him of the silly songs Aja had made up to cheer him up when he was upset. Kartikeya nodded to the girl who cleared her throat before addressing him directly. 'She came to me,' she said simply and Taraka stared at her, not quite understanding. *Who?*

'Your sister Ajamukhi came to me before she left to meet whatever awaited her on the other side,' she whispered. There were tears in her eyes and his own cheeks were wet with them. 'My father had locked me up in a cage. But she came in through the bars, so waiflike was her incorporeal form. It was for your sake that she did.'

'What did she say?' his gaze was fixed on her face, and he saw that there was nothing of her father there. Not that it mattered to him now.

'I was to tell you that even if you burnt down the three worlds or drowned it in blood, she would still love you to pieces. That you were a brute, a fool and a butchering pig but you would always be her beloved brother. She would remember even if all else forgot that you have a good heart that is capable of kindness and doing the right thing. That Soora, Simha and you meant everything to her. And always will.'

Taraka was weeping so hard none in the three worlds he had long terrorized would even recognize him. With tremulous fingers, she wiped away his tears. 'She made me memorize every single word. Before she went away, Aja told me that she hadn't wanted to come back because it was time to embark on a new journey filled with promise. But she had to come back. For you.'

They stood there for a long time. The girl. The boy. The peacock. And the former tyrant. Except he wasn't one anymore. His bear-like hands that had crushed the lives of so many were wrapped around the duo's feet in penitence. 'What happens to me now?' he asked, childlike and trusting.

Kartikeya smiled at him so kindly, his heart broke. 'That is entirely in your hands. You are free now.'

It was true, Taraka knew. He was free. And he knew exactly what it was he wanted to do. When Kartikeya raised him to his feet, they had spongy pads that would help him move with grace and precision over the rough terrain he was yet to traverse, his shoulders had broadened and they were a towering slab of grey granite. A huge trunk, the tip of which unrolled, gently touched the feet of the boy, whom he would love and revere forever more, before landing on the bowed head of the pretty little lady who had given him a reason to go on.

His large head seemed propped up by twin columns of ivory. Expansive grey ears flapped in the breeze and eyes that shone with emotion and intelligence were set in a seamed, weathered and noble face. He broke off a single tusk and laid it at their feet, in a touching gesture of gratitude. As he walked away in ponderous style, he looked back at them one last time, a stream of tears winding its way down the remaining tusk.

I will find a way to repay you for the kindness and favour you have shown me today. The words came out as a trumpet call that startled Devasena and Chitra, but Kartikeya understood. And then, Tarakasura was gone.

Sweet Sorrow

KARTIKEYA, DEVASENA AND Chitra tarried a bit longer at the site of the battle. They were silent as each processed what had been, was and would be. It was Devasena who spoke first. 'And to think that this is far from over. Soora and Simha will not take the loss of their brother lightly, especially as it comes on the heels of Ajamukhi's death. I daresay their response will be swift in coming and their retribution, deadly. My father and mother are still missing and I daresay they will resurface only after the remaining brothers no longer pose a threat to them.'

'Well, if Tarakasura's fate is any indication, then none of them need to worry,' Chitra was sardonic. 'Thanks to my Lord's brand of justice which comes with the promise of a happy ending, it is unlikely they will be condemned to an eternity of being punished for their sins.'

'Would you be able to do it then?' Kartikeya was curious, 'Inflict further pain on those who have been wounded and are hurting for a long time? Besides, Taraka was punished enough.

Nobody can save anybody from the consequences of their actions for better or worse; that is the way of it.'

Deva assumed he was talking to her. 'But you did save him!'

'I think it was you who did!'

Chitra shook his head at this soppy exchange. 'Still, it is good to know that even the evillest beings in the world are not exempt from redemption. I will be sure to remember it when seized with the urge to go on a mass-murdering spree and do my utmost to destroy everything in creation!'

Devasena rose to her feet. 'I must leave you now. It is time for me to retreat deep into the heart of Mother Earth, the parts that remain untouched by the ravages of war.'

'Don't go! Who will protect me from the wrath of Soora and Simha?' His tone was light but he wasn't fooling anybody. It was obvious that the thought of her impending departure grieved him deeply.

Devasena's smile was sad. 'When all this is over, we shall meet again. It was an honour to be by your side during your first battle. They say it is always the worst one. I will meet you again when it is time for your final battle. In the meantime, I will spend my days in the performance of penances, praying for your success.'

'Why don't you stay with my parents in Kailash? They will be happy to see you!'

Chitra snorted. He may be of Shiva's seed and perhaps the best of them all, and yet, when it came to some things, his innocence was ridiculous. Parvati would no doubt feel a whole gamut of emotions on finding out that her son had given his heart to Indra's daughter but happiness was extremely unlikely to be one of them. Karti surely knew of the bloody history between Indra and the Mother Goddess? But perhaps he'd rather he didn't know.

'I would like that very much,' she told him diplomatically, 'but it would be better if we were to meet them together. Until we meet again, I will spend every moment thinking of you, knowing that we are meant to be together.'

'When my duty is discharged, I will come for you and we shall be wed with the blessings of my parents. You will take your place by my side and we will be together forever more,' Kartikeya intoned with the solemnity of a binding oath.

Devasena embraced him then and he responded by throwing his arms around her. Holding her close, unwilling to ever let her go. 'I am so glad our paths crossed even though it was at the culmination of a profound tragedy. Every moment with you is a gift and a blessing for which I will always be grateful.'

Without warning, Devasena hugged Chitra too ignoring his squawk of protest and lordly disdain, unwilling to let her know that she had won his heart too. And just like that she was gone, disappearing into the darkness, exiting as suddenly from their lives as she had appeared.

'Well, she was right about one thing,' Chitra said. 'If your encounter with Taraka was draining in the extreme then your impending confrontation with the remainder of Maya's brood is likely to be every bit as bad.'

'Fortunately, I still have you by my side. If things get really bad, I'll be able to rely on your singing, which is far more painful than the most powerful weapon in any arsenal.'

'You *are* fortunate!' Chitra told him primly. 'Pretty ladies, even ones as nice as Devasena, will grow irksome once the first flush of passion is past and they may come and go. But your mount unlike your bride, will be with you forever!'

'And unlike my bride-to-be, you were irksome from the first,' Karti jested. Chitra decided that sarcasm of this sort deserved to be punished with stony silence and for that at least Kartikeya was glad. Together they rode into the sunset and towards a lion of a man, who had been sent forth to meet them on a mission of vengeance.

Hopping Mad

SOORA WAS ALL alone. Or in all accuracy, he was all that remained of his world. The former monarch was feeling more than a little morose and wondered how it had come to pass that he, who had once strode the three worlds like a colossus, had been reduced to something less than the meanest beggar whose greatest pleasure came from scratching at his sore riddled scrotum. Now he merely wandered the bleak terrain picking his way past treacherous rocks, loose stones and rubble that rolled underfoot tripping him up every once in a while.

His feet were torn and bleeding. Painful blisters had burst leaving gaping wounds that leaked pus. The rest of him wasn't in a much better shape. Attired in tattered rags, he couldn't remember the last time he had a bite to eat or a blessed drink. The flesh had melted off his bones leaving him emaciated and having responded unfavourably to the privations it had been forced to endure, his body was covered in scary looking bruises that looked life-threatening. In his present state, Soora would have given his life for a bowl of horse piss and his immortal soul for a handful of grain.

Instead all he had to fill his belly with were hearty helpings of regret, sorrow and abject despair. Soora was surprised a steady diet of the unpalatable trio hadn't driven him insane, although he had to concede that there was the distinct possibility that he had lost his mind. After all, no madman had ever been known to acquiesce that he was indeed stark, raving mad.

The only thing he had in abundance of was time and Soora liked to while it away by obsessively and masochistically going over events from the distant past that had led him irrevocably to the abyss before kicking him in the hindquarters and leaving him to his sad predicament. There was no comfort to be had from them but he was determined to make some sense of the epic tragedy that had swept through their lives.

When he was feeling marginally hopeful, he liked to wish for the impossible. Like getting his belongings back—kingdom, family and his mind. But he was a sensible man and had to concede that these were lost to him forever. All he could hope for now was death by the hand of Kartikeya after a glorious battle in which he acquitted himself with the brilliance that had formerly characterized his existence. The clash would be preserved in the annals of history for the rest of time and they would say he had taught Shiva's pup to raise his leg for a piss before his own grizzled head had rolled on the ground. If that was not a passing reasonable wish he did not know what was.

For the umpteenth time, he began sifting through the jumbled bits his increasingly unreliable memory had seen fit to retain in the hope of gaining a little perspective. Soora and Simha had been together when the news of Taraka's death and the decimation of his entire army had come to them. It boggled the mind but their enemies had seemingly done a thorough job of butchering their forces, taking care to ensure that none would survive to tell of the horrors that must have unfolded.

It was frustrating but all they had were wild rumours to work with. On Soora's orders everybody within a thousand miles from the scene of the battle were brought in for interrogation.

'I will find out the truth about my brother's demise if it means loosening every tongue in the three worlds with the gentle aid of heated tongs. If my suspicions are correct and Shiva's son had something to do with Taraka's death, then I will make him pay if it is the last thing I do!' he had bellowed at Simha who had been his usual circumspect self, thereby managing well and truly to get on his nerves.

From the accounts of the witnesses summoned, which were mostly garbled and incoherent, even by the standards of the worthless riff-raff they were, Soora and Simha managed to glean what information they could about the terrible fate that had overtaken their brother. Kartikeya had attacked Taraka from the heavens riding in a winged chariot of the purest gold. Indra and Vishnu had fought by his side along with Shiva's Ganas. Their brother had fought like the hero he had always been, vanquishing both the Wielder of the Thunderbolt and the Divine Protector, covering himself with glory.

Kartikeya had then challenged him to single combat. It was said that Bhoomi Devi trembled with fear as they duelled long and hard. Then, using fell tricks of sorcery and *maya*, he had learned from his mother, Shiva's son slew Taraka with his *vel*. The Kartikas who had accompanied him to battle feasted on the flesh of the fallen and grew drunk on their blood. Some mothers! Having been nursed by these monsters, it was small wonder that Kartikeya had a reputation for bloodthirstiness.

Soora remembered how utterly devastated he had been at the time. But that had been a while ago and he no longer had the energy for such intensity of feeling and could barely summon the strength to look back at the wretched remains of his past.

Aja and Taraka, the babies of the family, the ones he had sworn to protect had been snatched away from him by grisly death. The war showed no sign of abating and if anything, it seemed to have taken a malevolent life of its own as it raged across the three worlds consuming everybody and everything with a ferocious appetite. It was clearly the beginning of the end and every ominous omen seemed to indicate as much.

Cows no longer gave milk and animals to be butchered for meat seemed stricken with a strange illness that saw their entrails filled to bursting with white worms. Even the carrion birds would not go near the carcasses or peck at the contaminated insides. Babies died in the womb or were born afflicted with severe deformities. It was said that the Kartikas were attacking the little ones and would not stop till they had snuffed out all life.

Worse, they were no closer to apprehending Indra than they had been when it had all gone to hell. Soora had not thought it was possible for things to become even more wretched and had steeled himself to ride out the storm. But he had been hopelessly wrong. The situation had spiralled out of control and he had found himself sinking deeper and deeper into a morass from which there had been no escape.

It had never been Soora's intention to fight a child. But Taraka's death had changed everything and he had no choice but to declare war on Shiva's son. Simha had joined him in Mahendrapuri. Their troops had burnt down every single temple in the three worlds after stripping them of valuables and smashing the idols to smithereens. Devotees who protested the sacrilege and wished to die for their faith were allowed to do so with alacrity.

Kartikeya had shown up at the gates then with an army cobbled together from the wickedest of evil elements who had been banished to the extreme outposts of the universe unfit even to inhabit Yama's thousand hells exclusively reserved as it was for the foulest and most diabolical of creatures. Bhootaganas and Dakinis, hand-picked from the bloodthirsty legions who made up the devotees of Shiva and Shakti as well as a terrifying assortment of supernatural entities—ghosts, ghouls, giants, fiends and wraiths rounded out the dread legions from a nightmare.

The three worlds had never before seen such a nefarious force, capable of razing entire worlds to the ground. Needless to say, the remains of Soora and Simha's army had been at a complete disadvantage. In retrospect their desperate attempts to mount a semblance of resistance against the avalanche that had mowed them down had been laughable, if hardly a laughing matter.

Abominations covered in boils that oozed foul effluence descended on them like pestilential insects, bringing with them the blight of rot, decay and illness, afflicting the healthiest and heartiest among them. So many had sickened, dying in agony, sapped of strength and robbed of the will to live, taking the helpless healers whose best had not been enough with them into the abyss of certain death.

Ghostly apparitions launched surprise attacks sneaking up

on them, preying on the minds of hapless victims who would die screaming in terror, as their worst fears took shape and hounded them to madness. Unable to deal with their addled brains, many had chosen to put an end to it by taking their own lives.

Monsters who breathed fire and smoke, generated enough flame and heat, burning through stone, brick, mortar and life as though they were little more than kindling, till all of civilization was reduced to an enormous funeral pyre that demanded more and more of the living as well as the possessions they held dear.

Black clouds engulfed the blue of the heavens, and a toxic sulphurous mist descended shrouding everything in darkness, cutting off all sources of light. Trees, plants, flowers and flora of every type died in alarming numbers. Life-giving sources of water were befouled and rendered putrid, killing the fish that floated, stinking and bloated to the surface. Scorched carcasses of winged creatures dropped out of the skies like stones and acid rain had finished off the remaining attempts of life to renew itself.

Spirit creatures went to work on the handful of survivors, butchering them with nasty efficiency, wielding their axes, daggers, pikes, war hammers, clubs and staves with gay abandon, giving generously their grisly gift for gore. Then came the feeders with serrated teeth and burning red eyes that could take apart the toughest armour with ease before feeding on the hearts, souls and mortal remains of the deceased, finding a way to violate those beyond reach.

The Giants had been the fiercest combatants and they came to administer the finishing touches on his empire rent apart by war and pestilence, already twitching in its death throes. Even so, it took years of burning and slaughter before it was all over.

When the end came, it was almost a relief.

Everybody he loved had died. Soora had tried his utmost to hold onto them but the harder he held on to them, the quicker they died. Banugopan, his favourite son, had been overwhelmed by an abhorrent creature with filthy claws that had somehow paralyzed him before finishing him off at leisure, while Soora watched, paralyzed himself but not devoid of sensation, if the pain of bereavement that had lacerated his soul was any indication.

His remaining sons, wives, and daughters had fared no better and the minutiae of their tragic demise had come close to driving him to insanity. Soora's favourite wife of long years was a gentle soul but she had demanded and received from him the gift of a merciful death. He wished often that he had taken that route himself.

It was Simha's fate that had hit him the hardest. His brother was more precious to him than all the treasures he had accumulated and he would have gladly traded his eyes, limbs and very life to have him back. The worst was not knowing what had become of him. Simha had been in the thick of fighting and a gaggle of viragoes with forked tongues had him surrounded. Soora had seen that his brother was pulling his punches on account of the fact that it went against his code of honour to handle a woman roughly.

'They are vicious killers, Simha! Show them no mercy for you will receive none from them!'

His brother seemed not to have heard. The vile women had made way for Kartikeya who had called out to Simha no doubt challenging him to single combat. He had wanted to fight his way past the press to reach his brother but by the time he fought his way clear, Simha was gone and so was his killer. If he didn't know better he would have thought they hadn't been there in the first place.

Soora saw them both in his dreams though. Or at least he thought he did. A lion charged at him every time slumber had gathered him in his embrace. But he was not afraid. For in its majestic countenance and feral eyes, he saw his brother. 'Soora…' a voice rasped in his ear, 'I am close.'

The words were a panacea for the strife that beset his soul and Soora always reached out to the other half of his heart. But then he saw her—a frightful Goddess of fearsome aspect with a thousand arms wielding weapons in each and an aura so powerful that it repelled his touch and sent him reeling away, abashed and in tears. She sat astride Simha and they rode off into the distance together. He would wake up screaming and in tears.

Shiva's son called to him. But he wished to have nothing to do with the one who had murdered his brothers. He did not mind the peacock though. Sometimes he saw the bird dancing in the rain, its glorious feathers spread out in a riot of colour. The very sight made his heart lift and he felt his cares disappear as he too joined in the exuberance and revelled in the rejuvenating showers.

Soora shook his head trying in vain to clear the cobwebs in his head that clouded his thinking. No matter how many times he prowled the corridors of conscious memory, it was hard to make sense of any of it. He stared long and hard at the godforsaken terrain that was all that was left. This frightful ordeal had taken everything from him and he knew that he would not last long. It was the most heartening thought he had had in ages. His great spirit quivered in resignation and he sank to his knees, throwing up his hands in surrender.

Closure

$\mathcal{I}$T WAS THE worst of times and the weakest he had ever been. The horrors he had experienced had left him crippled. But worst of all was the overwhelming fear that assailed him in brutal waves. It was at the very nadir of his hopelessness and agony that Shiva's son came for him, bringing with him the hint of a promise and a whiff of hope—that everlasting joy was not only possible but entirely within his grasp.

As Kartikeya approached, the veils of darkness seemed to part and the golden rays of the sun which Soora had believed lost to him forever bathed the lad with its radiance, and warmed his own frozen core. More importantly, splinters appeared on the solid wall of fear that held him constricted and he welcomed the return of his sense of well-being as his terrors dissipated with every step the one they called by many names took to close the distance between them.

Soora stared as he approached on foot, mesmerized by those arresting features and charming ringlets. He had heard that the Devas, in a bid to bribe him to join their cause, had looted Kubera's treasury and bestowed upon him the fabled wonders that had been housed within. But this boy wore no ornaments and was clothed in little more than the animal skins favoured by his father; not that he needed rich garments or ostentatious jewellery to enhance that which nature had already bestowed upon him in such abundance.

He carried no weapons, not even the dreadful *vel* that had supposedly pierced Taraka's heart. Nor anything from the celestial armoury which the Devas had allegedly emptied to equip him with. There was no trace of his pretty peacock either, notorious for its penchant for devouring snakes. Apparently, its horrendous cries could incapacitate all those within hearing range who would then die trying to staunch their bleeding ears.

'What have you done to my brothers?' Soora began, his voice hoarse from disuse, trying in vain to fan the flames of his anger before giving up. Somehow in the presence of this strange and enigmatic being, it was hard to feel anything but good.

'If I told you what has become of them would you take my word for it? Would you be able to believe?' Kartikeya queried. 'I doubt it, but set your mind at ease! Your brothers voluntarily made the choices they could live with by opting to leave behind the confines of a limit-filled existence and the endless violence that has shadowed them on this side of death.'

'It is hard to even imagine that Taraka invited you to strike him dead. Or that Simha willingly abandoned me to subject himself to whatever torture you devised for him. So you will forgive me for not believing you.' Soora had wanted to coat his words with heavy irony but it came out more curious than scathing.

'I knew you wouldn't believe me!' A boyish grin lit up that face which could never be anything but dear. Clearly, he loved being proved right. 'As you know, Taraka was ruled by his uncontrollable passions. By their very nature, these could never ever be fully assuaged. Every time he indulged them, all he succeeded in doing was to inflame them further, leaving him aching and empty. At the very root of the violence that tinged everything he did was Taraka himself and the wounds he carried, many of which were admittedly self-inflicted.'

'He was capable of selfless love too!'

Soora was surprised when Kartikeya nodded in agreement. 'In the end, it was what saved him. It was love that healed all that was broken and wounded inside him.' Soora recognized in those words the timbre of a truth that could not be denied. And he was grateful to whatever it had taken to make him believe. But he needed more.

'Simha was not governed by the baseness of primitive needs and urges,' Soora argued, but without any rancour. 'None in the three worlds had a bigger heart or a more beautiful soul. What has become of him? Say what you will but he does not deserve the ignominy of death, even if it is by your hand, for his enemies have put you up to it. They have done everything in their power to spread calumny and dishonour his memory. History will remember him as an evil villain and he was anything but. Where is the justice in all of this?'

'You do know what has become of Simhamukha.' It was a reprimand but so gentle it felt like a caress. 'And after everything you have seen, I am surprised you are still concerned with the lies, distortions and stories of history, though I will admit that they can be most entertaining and occasionally even educational. You are right about Simha, the Lionhearted, though. He lived his life with grace and goodness, deriving whatever joy he could even during troubled times and did his best to spread it around. Ultimately though, he knew enough not to become too enamoured with the encumbrances that most cling to and sought instead to move on to something better that was just beyond his self.'

'How could he have moved on to something better when you have condemned him to servitude? Simha abhorred destruction but now he is enslaved within the form of a lion, noble beast though it may be, by a dreaded Goddess, the mysterious and cruel one they call Durga and will be forced to carry her into endless wars of attrition,' Soora could not stop himself from grousing. 'My brother couldn't possibly want to spend eternity with one who thrives on the blood of her victims.'

'Simha wouldn't be happy to hear such an atrociously inaccurate description of the Goddess Durga, whose capacity for compassion is unmatched. Mahishasura himself would attest to that though legend has it that she split him asunder.' It was another of those rebukes which somehow did not sting, 'And you accuse the Devas of spreading fanciful tales lacking in veracity! Simha wanted to consecrate himself in service to the Mother Goddess and would no doubt tell you that it is the best decision he has ever made. Know that and be reassured.'

Soora would have loved to feel assured but he wasn't quite there and he said as much to his new friend, 'If you think Taraka and Simha have done well by themselves and are as happy as they are ever going to be, then your word is good enough for me. And yet, I cannot help but be angered that Ajamukhi's brutal murder has gone unavenged. Now that my brothers and I are no more, Indra, the covetous coward will get his greedy, grasping paws on the crown and throne he loves so well. It always did gall me that the perfidious perpetrator of all things evil winds up getting everything his treacherous excuse for a heart desires.'

Kartikeya shook his head as if Soora himself was the precocious child, naïve and unfamiliar with the workings of the universe. 'Now you are the one who is persisting in being perverse! Even if Indra were to get the crown and throne that you yourself owned, surely you are aware that he would derive as much happiness from those worthless baubles as you yourself did, which, if memory serves, was next to nothing? His need for power is every bit as misguided as your quest for revenge and is likely to yield the exact same empty rewards.'

'I won't blame you if you feel a sudden urge to impale me with your *vel*,' Soora persisted, 'but there are many more burning questions that I would like answered.'

'You are safe from my weapons,' Kartikeya grinned at him and it felt like a blessing which Soora was delighted to receive. 'I daresay I am getting used to the barrage of words that you always feel the need to give voice to even if others are less kindly disposed towards this particular attribute of yours.'

'It bothers me to no end that precious life and bonds of love are so tenuous and fragile. Losing a loved one or watching the elements lash out arbitrarily in the form of natural disasters like earthquakes, erupting volcanoes, floods, tornadoes and claiming lives at an alarming rate is awful enough, but worst of all is the conscious decision made by those of us who wield power to kill those who look to us for succour and sustenance. The guilt is something that can scarce be borne and I cannot help thinking that my actions which had such cataclysmic consequence are beyond the reach of forgiveness.'

Soora fell silent when he looked back on his own decision to go to war to assuage his personal grief. It had directly contributed to the madness that had engulfed them all and destroyed life as he knew it. Profound regret coursed through his being and he envied Kartikeya his serenity, though the power he wielded was far greater than his own and had wreaked more havoc than even the excesses of the Devas and Asuras combined.

'You are guilty too,' he said tremulously, horrified at his own daring which he was sure would be the death of him. 'Your actions too have led to immense damage. The mighty deeds you will no doubt be extolled for have claimed innocent lives too!'

'My mother is innocent too and my first allegiance will always be to her,' Kartikeya said, smiling at the look of puzzlement on Soora's face. 'Bhoomi Devi gives unstintingly of her bounty and yet the life forms she sustains so lovingly take from her without ever bothering to care for her well-being or repay her generosity with care and consideration. In the end they are victims of their own actions and if it is blood and death that will bring Mother Earth back to life, then it is a price that has to be paid.'

Soora nodded, with a hint of the comprehension he had long sought. While it was true that he couldn't see things with crystal clarity he was glad that mercifully, the black fugue of his confusion had been lifted. Besides, he was more grateful than he could say for the gracious explanation which he knew was a mark of high favour. If everything he had undergone had been merely so he could be a part of this conversation, then he would gladly go through it all again. Perhaps it was the maddest, most audacious thought he had ever had; it was, nevertheless, how he felt. They sat in companionable silence for long moments. Soora felt so good, he could scarcely believe it, especially since he had been at the end of his rope and dangerously close to giving up so very recently. In fact, it all seemed funny to him in retrospect and more than a little absurd.

Finally, reposing within the comforting aura of the God who was by his side, he asked the question his brothers had before him, 'What happens to me now? Are you sure you will not rend me in two and grant me the gift of oblivion?'

'Is that what you really want? Oblivion?' Kartikeya teased. 'You would hate an eternity of enforced tranquillity and keeping still! And I think we have both had enough of rending and tearing.'

'You are not getting off that easily,' Soora persisted, 'tell me what is to become of me? You did say that my brothers were given a choice. Does that mean I get to choose as well? I agree about the rending and tearing... No more claws and teeth for me! But that said, I am not entirely sure about what to do next. To be honest, I am perfectly content right now and would rather not change anything.'

'It is good to know that! Especially since you have already made your choice. And what is going to happen to you has already happened.' Kartikeya was smiling and it was a beautiful sight. 'You decided that a pretty plumage and a beak are far superior to more predatory embellishments and accoutrements which, as you rightly pointed out, are made for warlike purposes. It just took some time to make your peace with everything but I think you are ready now.'

And finally, it was all crystal clear. He looked down at himself and understood. Kartikeya was walking away and he flapped his gorgeous feathers to catch up with him. He decided that it wasn't the worst thing that had happened to him and as things stood he had no cause for complaint.

'It is too bad that when the stirring saga of Soorapadma is told in the ages to come, they will leave out the good parts and content themselves with saying something far-fetched—that you broke me in half and used the parts to make your vehicle and decorate your flag,' he groused, deciding that he liked how tuneful he sounded.

'It is not too bad as far as stories go and most manage to retain the salient points,' Karti countered. 'Besides, if you keep up with the incessant chatter, you can count on me doing just that and it will be no more than what you deserve.'

A Family Reunion

𝒫ARVATI HAD SWORN that she would not make a sorry spectacle of herself when her son was returned to her. But on seeing her little boy all grown up and resplendent from his recent triumphs, she began weeping much to the amusement of her Lord and dear husband. He in turn was looking even prouder than the peacock their son rode on.

Leaping off his mount, he made straight for his parents, engulfing them in a bear hug which knocked the breath out of her chest which was already filled to bursting with love for her handsome and noble boy. It was good to have him back.

'My Karti is the finest specimen of Godhood,' Parvati had intoned in rapturous tones to Shiva when he had been away, 'and I am not saying that just because I am his mother.'

Shiva rolled his eyes, 'Now you sound like every mother on the three worlds who insists her son is the very epitome of perfection even if he is guilty of being vile, treacherous or extraordinarily ordinary.'

'That only proves my point,' she had insisted. 'My son is neither vile, treacherous, nor ordinary. He has performed truly extraordinary deeds and it isn't his good looks, expertise with weaponry and other talents that set him apart, prodigious though they may be. It is his innate goodness and endless capacity for kindness as well as compassion. If everything in the three worlds, possessed of a male member, including present company, were to emulate him then we would not have to deal with half the problems we are currently dealing with.'

Shiva had laughed. His wife was usually hilarious when hyperbolic but he was mildly worried that she loved the boy a little too fiercely for her own good. Or his. And with good reason. He knew what it was like to be at the giving and receiving end of a love so vehement that it was almost violent. Parvati had found herself disillusioned when she discovered that perfection in love or marriage was never meant to last. She had dealt with the persistent dissatisfaction by drowning her marital disappointment in the deluge of her overpowering love for dear Kartikeya.

I hope she is able to deal with the double dose of disenchantment better than I think she will, Shiva mused, not without a touch of misgiving.

Now that Karti had returned to them, Shiva hoped they could look forward to a little peace and quiet on the family front. In the beginning at least, that was the case and they all got a taste of delicious domestic bliss. Karti doted on his mother and they spent a lot of quality time together. He even took her for a ride on his precious peacock and they had flown all over the three worlds taking in the evidence of the traumatic ordeal that Bhoomi Devi had been through.

'You have done a good job, Karti!' she had patted him on

the shoulder. 'All the rot and decay that had set in deep within Bhoomi Devi's core has been burnt away during the course of the tumultuous events that rocked the three worlds. She has also been culled of the more vicious parasites that besieged her person.'

'Even knowing all this, it grieves me to see her in this state,' Karti said. 'Ashes don't suit her very well. It would please me to see her in the full bloom of her beauty.'

'All males, irrespective of the species they belong to, like their females to be lush and fertile. Why should you be any different?' she replied drily and with the slightest touch of asperity at this certain indicator that Karti was no longer a boy. 'But don't you worry. It is only a matter of time before she regenerates and is restored to her full splendour. And I daresay you will have a part in it, for you have served her well and she loves you almost as much as I do.'

Despite the excessive bonding with his mother, Shiva was not surprised when his boy chose him to broach a rather delicate subject with. He had sensed Karti's restlessness and could hazard a guess as to what was at the root of it. They were on one of their jaunts together and had managed to give their devotees and attendants the slip. These had burgeoned in numbers ever since Karti's recent deeds had come to light. There were many who were besotted with him and had taken to worshipping him with lavish displays of love and affection.

Karti was still getting used to it but he seemed to be handling all the adulation with surprising maturity. The Devas were among the most fervent of his admirers. They were so grateful to him for freeing them from the clutches of Maya's sons, it was beyond pathetic. Already he was at the epicentre of their plans to reclaim their glory days.

Nandi had reported that since Indra and his wife had not yet seen fit to grace the three worlds with their presence, the Devas wished to crown him as their King. Thanks to Parvati's curse, none of them had children so they wished for the new ruler to be joined in holy matrimony with their former ruler's daughter, Devasena. Their Princess had apparently surfaced and appeared busily engaged in the revival of an ailing Bhoomi Devi. He had no doubt that his son would be more than happy to accede to the latter half of their plan but his wife would no doubt prise open his third eye and incinerate the lot of them before allowing such a thing to happen.

Both of them had been going over their thoughts in silence. Karti broke it first, 'Devasena helped me in the rather delicate matter with Taraka. I thought that he may have to be put down but she showed me a better way. The Princess defied her father to do it and I swore to find her after the war. The time has come for me to honour my promise. But I am getting the unshakeable feeling that Mother will be most opposed towards such a course of action.'

'You suppose right. Your mother will most certainly oppose your decision to go back to Indra's daughter. Her exact words were that you would do such a thing only over her dead body,' Shiva said without preamble.

'But why?' Karti wanted to know. 'Devasena has done nothing to incur this kind of dislike.'

'Absolutely nothing,' Shiva agreed, 'except be born as Indra's daughter. And I am fully aware that it is hardly her fault, but your mother tends to be unreasonable where the Wielder of the Thunderbolt is concerned. Their enmity goes back a long way in time and she has neither forgotten nor forgiven him.'

'Do tell me all about it,' Karti requested. His forehead was scrunched up the way it usually was when he was somewhat perturbed. He was starting to think Devasena was about the only good thing Indra had ever had a hand in.

'It all started with the Goddess of Dawn,' Shiva replied, a faraway look in his eyes. 'Her name was Usas. She was something special—the very first manifestation of the sacred feminine. The three worlds have never recovered from her loss and with good reason, for she was the most benevolent of them all. Mortal and immortal loved her beyond reason and Indra envied the power she wielded over the hearts of all.

'Unfortunately, she was the victim of the first crime. Brahma had long harboured a forbidden passion for her and one day, he waylaid and violated her. Rudra went to her rescue but sensing that she was traumatized and vulnerable, Indra accused her of seducing her father and chased the Goddess from the heavens with his thunderbolt. She withdrew into the fires of *prakriti* to nurse her wounds and later re-emerged in a more formidable avatar. Usas herself was seen no more. Yet the first crime against the sacred feminine continues to have repercussions, making it all the more unforgivable, because a precedent had been set. Those belonging to the gentler sex continue to be victimized, leading to considerable ill-will between men and women. The seeds for the gender wars were planted and we continue to reap the bitter harvest.'

Karti shook his head in disgust. 'I did not know this! How unspeakably tragic! Brahma and Indra should have been castrated and exiled to the wildest reaches of Bhoomi Devi. They should not have gone unpunished!'

'None are exempt from the consequence of their deeds,' Shiva was dead serious. 'By daring to abuse a potent manifestation of Shakti without whom none, including myself, can exist, they have cursed themselves and have well and truly earned the comeuppance that will eventually catch up with them. Their powers have dwindled into insignificance over the ages and neither can bring himself to swallow the foul-tasting broth they brewed for themselves.'

'It is quite the story,' Karti shuddered with outrage. 'I thought you were going to tell me about the time Brahma lusted after Shakti and profaned the occasion of your wedding to her, by shedding his seed. Or about Daksha's ill-fated *yagna*, where Shakti immolated herself, unable to bear the disrespect shown to you and the abuse meted out to her by Indra and the Devas who resented her power.'

Karti stopped when he saw the tears coursing down his father's cheeks. It moved him deeply to see that after all this time, Shiva could be so affected by the loss of his Shakti. He had heard that his father had been demented with grief and was never the same without his one true love.

'It wasn't about her power alone,' Shiva spoke so softly, he may well have been speaking to himself, 'and it certainly wasn't about Daksha, Brahma, Indra or the others. We loved each other. Always did. A little too much in fact. To the exclusion of all else including our very selves. It reached a point where neither of us knew where Shiva began and Shakti ended or the other way around. We were one and same. Our union was one that transcended everything including bliss and happiness.'

He paused, lost in the memories of a wondrous time when he had the pluck to surrender everything he was to love. Karti held his breath, suddenly terrified for he knew what was coming. 'It should have ended there and neither of us would have complained. But time is forever without a beginning or an end, which, ironically enough, is why nothing lasts forever. I think we both began to miss the heady passion of our early days and it tarnished our tranquillity, made our bliss banal and negated the nothingness that comes with being part of a whole.'

Karti shuddered and tried not to choke on his tears. Shiva went on, pushing past his own pain, needing to lance the poison from an old wound that still bled. 'In the end, we loved each other too much for our own good and we missed being ourselves. Secretly, we craved the succour of solitude and the ability to feel something. Anything. Having completed each other, perversely we longed to feel incomplete so that we could once again be part of the joyous process of discovering true love. In the end, overwhelmed by the sheer perfection of belonging, scared senseless by its implications for our independence, we allowed ourselves to be torn apart. And because she was always the tougher of us, it was she who bore the brunt of it all.'

'You miss her, don't you?' Karti asked him. 'I know that Shakti promised to come back to you and she kept her word, returning to your side as Parvati. And yet, it can never be quite the same, can it?'

'I am not complaining,' Shiva smiled. 'Having lost her once, I am glad to have my love and life returned to me. The pain of parting and aching emptiness have enhanced the pleasures of togetherness a hundredfold. Besides, perfection can never hope to sustain itself in perpetuity, which is why this time round, I am grateful for the niggling imperfections which make the rare moments of perfection all the more valuable.'

Impulsively, Karti threw his arms around his father's neck, making the serpents hiss in outrage. When he drew back, his hair was slicked back with Ganga's waters. 'Be sure to tell this story to Mother someday. It will help her appreciate any glaring imperfections in her firstborn.'

Shiva did not reply to that. And they walked home in silence. Karti couldn't help thinking that for the rest of time he wouldn't forget the honour his father had done him by sharing the secrets of his heart. Correctly, he intuited that none before him had had the same privilege. Not even his mother. His heart swelled with pride. An annoying voice at the back of his heart informed him that it would be all the better positioned for a pin to burst it asunder.

Apprehension filled him as he mused on the loaded conversation he needed to have with Parvati, especially in light of everything Shiva had told him. It did not help that Indra had incurred his mother's ire in recent times by interfering with the process that had led to his own birth. He sighed aloud. What an unholy mess! And now his mother's hatred towards Indra extended to dear Devasena as well. Already he missed her more than he could bear and could hardly wait to see her again.

Shiva sighed, imitating him, and punched him lightly on the shoulder. 'There is no need to look so demoralized, son. We will talk to your mother together. She has been known to listen to reason on occasion.' *Though it is too bad mothers are incapable of being reasonable when it comes to their precious sons*, he amended silently to himself.

Karti seemed to share his misgivings and he sighed again. 'Mother's misgivings regarding Indra are well founded and she probably just needs a little time to wrap her head around accepting Indra's daughter as her daughter-in-law. I am sure she will come around eventually. It is hard not to love Devasena once you get to know her.'

'No doubt!' his father agreed and it took considerable effort but Karti managed not to hear the mild sarcasm.

Parvati took one look at the duo and her expression turned stony. She had anticipated just this eventuality and instructed her husband to exercise his best efforts towards dissuading their son from persisting in this foolishness. But from their jointly mutinous expressions, she sensed that Shiva had been singularly ineffective. Not only had he failed to convince their son, but allowed himself to be convinced that Karti's misplaced feelings for their enemy's brat wasn't downright dangerous. Sometimes Shiva made her so angry!

Fortunately, Parvati had known better than to rely entirely on him. Anticipating his lack of perspicacity in the matter, she had arranged for certain measures to be implemented to protect her son from the wiles of strumpets who dared to believe themselves worthy of him.

Neither seemed willing to speak up and they kept nudging each other, no doubt foolishly supposing themselves to be subtle and unobtrusive. It was most irksome and she tried to keep her rising temper in check.

In as level a voice as she could manage, Parvati spoke first, 'As you both know, the Devas are keen that Karti become their ruler, since Indra remains in hiding though his daughter seems to be doing everything possible to draw attention to herself. They are dangling the poisoned fruit from his loins as bait, no doubt hoping you will bite. Unfortunately for them, I raised you to be smarter than that.'

Karti winced but Parvati could not help noticing the resolve in his eyes, and felt a flutter in her heart. 'I do not seek to rule over anybody as you well know, Mother. The mortals have evolved faster than anybody expected and they don't need the immortals to watch over them anymore. Besides, as recent events have indicated, they are better off without the deadly power games between the Devas and Asuras. A bifurcation of the two realms is inevitable and is the need of the hour. The Devas are resisting, knowing that it is the worship of the mortals and their faith in them which lends them their own power. My taking over at the helm will only interfere with this process. However…'

'I am glad to hear that, but there is more to be considered. The very fact that the Devas seek to install you on their throne places you in mortal peril. Indra will fight tooth and nail to regain his former glory and restore the Devas to the exalted station they have long enjoyed. He will consider you a threat and will stop at nothing to make sure that you do not usurp his precious position.'

'He is welcome to try,' Karti said with supreme nonchalance, 'and I will be glad to settle the score with him. I owe it to Soora, Simha, Taraka and Ajamukhi.'

'And what of his daughter?' she asked caustically. 'Indra is not above using her to suit his needs and will you oblige him by allowing lust to cloud your vision?' The moment she heard the words she had uttered, Parvati wished she could take them back. There was hurt in her son's eyes and it pained her to know that she was entirely responsible.

'From what I hear, she is estranged from her father. Apparently, he locked her up in a cage when she failed to fall in with his plans,' Shiva pitched in helpfully. 'What's more, she even helped Karti here kill with kindness, or something every bit as touching.'

Mother and son did not crack a smile. Parvati was furious with Shiva for the show of support for Karti's plans in the face of her opposition. How like him to play the hero aiding in his son's forbidden love, leaving her to do what needed to be done and making her out to be the villain! Even so, unlike him, she had the nerve to do what a parent must. She turned the full force of her formidable glare on Karti, who didn't flinch or budge an inch.

Shiva shook his head in silent despair. Here, he had thought his fights with his consort were painful in the extreme, but they were not a patch on this particular clash. He shuddered on behalf of his son who was being pulled in two different directions by his beloved mother and chosen wife. The Destroyer thought fondly of a time when he had remained immersed in meditation, far removed from domestic cares. And there were many who wondered why ascetics turned their backs on the promise of pleasure and fulfilment to spend their days enduring intense privation, while suspended from the ankles and covered in their own filth, allowing fire ants to march up their spines.

Shiva tried appealing to Karti, 'Are you certain that romance and marriage will be the best fit for you, my boy? Take it from one who has been there and done all that. Marriage is to lust, what death is to life. It is well and good to fall deeply in love but handcuffing yourself to the object of your affection is never a good idea.'

Karti managed a small smile which did nothing to take the edge off the fact that his loving wife was looking daggers at him. 'I daresay you are right, but it will not make me change my mind. I made a promise to Princess Devasena and I intend to honour it. Besides, we are made for each other, rather like the two of you.'

'It is not the same thing!' Parvati was shaking with rage at being compared with one whose name she wouldn't utter even in her own mind. 'My father, the great Himavan, is a good soul who loves and respects my husband. In this case, there is bad blood between our families and no good can from such a union, not the least because that creature's father wants you dead. If you trust the judgement of your mother who loves you above all else and wants nothing but the best for her, son, you will desist with this foolhardiness and forget the girl.'

'I love you above all else and you do me an injustice by questioning my feelings for you. But I will not be a worthy son to the Goddess Parvati if I were to cast off one who I am beholden to!' Karti was equally adamant.

'Far be it for me to stop you from following the dictates of your heart, but know that Indra's daughter is not welcome here and never will be.'

To her surprise, he smiled. It was a smile full of the cheeky insouciance. 'You will change your mind, mother. Devasena is a part of me, and you love me, above all else. Even more than your Shiva. And you can never stop yourself from loving such an integral part of me.'

He threw his arms around her and held her tight, refusing to let go till she relented as he knew she would and hugged him back. 'I will watch over you,' she murmured, 'and pray that your mind which is clouded with the storm clouds of desire for the damnable will be cleared soon by the light of wisdom.'

There were fresh tears in her eyes as Karti bid farewell to his father, noting that he was now almost as tall as Shiva and departed on his peacock. Someday she would wring that damned bird's neck to stop it from carrying him away from her.

'That did not go as badly as I thought it would.' Shiva was watching her intently and Parvati refused to meet his gaze. 'It is not at all like you to agree to disagree and leave things be.'

'I'll be damned before allowing that little hussy to come between me and my son.' She murmured, 'Besides, good luck to him, finding her.'

Shiva frowned, 'What have you done? Try to remember that he is our dear son and you love him nearly as much as you love me. Can you believe the temerity of that little rapscallion daring to presume that you could possibly care more about him than me? Be that as it may, please tell me you haven't done something we will both regret.'

'All I have done has been done keeping the best interests of my son in mind. And after all this time, I think I have the right to your trust.' It was said with magnificent disdain and in a tone that would brook no further argument.

His worst suspicions were now confirmed. This little kerfuffle between Parvati was about to get so much worse. And there would be a lot of collateral damage, starting with his own self before the thrice-damned thing could be sorted out and smoothed over. Shiva could not help wondering if this girl was even worth all this trouble. It bothered him that his son was showing such extraordinary haste in rushing off to ensnare himself within the suffocating confines of holy matrimony and its attendant sorrows.

Still, it was Kartikeya's decision to make and unlike his wife, he was determined not to interfere. Shiva could not help being pleased with the remarkable maturity and wisdom his son was showing in this delicate matter. Glancing pityingly at his wife who was still staring into the distance lost in thoughts of her son, he hoped for the sake of their little family that some of his surpassing good sense would rub off on her.

Waylaid by Love and Lust

KARTIKEYA HAD EVERY intention of making his way towards Devasena. In fact, he could not wait to tell her everything that had happened since they last met. It bothered him a little that his mother had not taken to her future daughter-in-law or been remotely enthused at the prospect of including her in their family.

'She will come around,' he said aloud. Chitra snorted loudly and Karti could not be sure but it may have been his way of telling him exactly what he thought of such excessive optimism. 'Mother and Devasena do not have to love each other. I'll happily settle for mutual politeness which, I am certain, will turn into something more cordial with time. Besides, no relationship is perfect and without exception all will have its share of good as well as bad moments.'

'That's right, keep hoping for the best,' Chitra said with a smirk. 'But I think your father is right. For someone who is happily married, he does not seem to think there is much to recommend it. Nothing would ever convince me to trade my freedom and handcuff myself to a peahen, even if she is the most appealing. Hatching eggs and putting up with peachicks every bit as vain and wilful as I am is hardly my definition of a good time.'

Karti was vaguely troubled. He had always assumed that his mother and father were as happy as it was possible to be. Yet, Chitra was right. The cracks were showing. Restlessly, his eyes scanned the horizon. He wondered if he could convince his uncle Vishnu to let him borrow Garuda in exchange for his own loquacious mount. Where was Devasena? He hoped to find her sooner rather than later.

But they found him first and surged towards him in an almighty rush. Even Chitra was overawed into silence at the sheer multitudes that were converging upon them in wave after wave. All were calling out to him in a rhapsody of frenzied emotion that seemed to have equal parts anguish and elation. Kartikeya felt himself respond. They pooled around him as he landed in their midst, separating him from Chitra and obstructing the way forward.

It was impossible to count their numbers. There appeared to be tens of thousands, perhaps even millions of them. They were of all shapes and sizes, diverse as the stars in the sky, all of varying origin. There were those who were so beautiful, they took his breath away. Many more were of fearsome aspect and not easy to look upon. Some were in the full bloom of youth, others were old and hoary.

He heard the gentle tinkle of anklets, clinking of bangles, swishing of clothing, and twirling of flamboyant tails. The many voices clamouring for his attention. There were flashes of colour with the preening of brightly coloured plumage, and his senses tingled as they gathered around him drawn to the warmth of the energy emanating from him.

Among those who thronged about him, there were those who had had their homes in the heavens, in the celestial regions. They had been the wives and lovers of Gods accustomed to wallowing in the lap of luxury, having lived in the finest of palaces where the silverware was solid gold. Once upon a time, they had been lovely to look upon for they had bedecked themselves with gold cloth and adorned themselves with exquisite pieces of priceless jewellery. But that had been before the war. And Parvati's curse.

'The war took everything from us,' they wailed. 'We were kidnapped and defiled by Taraka. Goddess Parvati punished us for the sins of our husbands and said that we will remain barren forever more. Taraka is no more, leaving us bereft of pleasure and pain both. We will not go back to our husbands. They left us to our fates and we will leave them to theirs. We belong to you now, do as you will with us!'

Maidens from the seas and mountains, traditional abode of the Asuras, addressed him, 'Our men have been vanquished in the great war. The victors were not content to destroy them once. By violating us repeatedly they sought to defeat and humiliate their foes over and over again. Nothing remains of our homes and lives. You are all we have.'

There were those of humbler origin belonging to the realms of mortals, 'The war took everything from us too—husband, home, and honour. Men, Gods and beasts, they were not content with shedding blood. No! They were not, they parted the pillars of our thighs, spilled their seed, profaning us! Now we are torn and bleeding. There is nothing but devastation for us to return to. We will not go back! Save us!'

More and more gathered around him. All spoke a different tongue and they came from all over the three worlds. But they said the same things over and over again. Winged creatures and aerial nymphs hovered over him, teasing him with silken caresses. Water sprites brushed against him with their scaled bodies that had tails and fins instead of feet. Spirits of the land and forest with talons and protuberant lips pushed past the others to get closer.

Wraiths and ghosts floated about, singing their doleful songs of woe. 'War tore the life from us but they failed to set us free. So we have wandered the three realms with nowhere to go, searching endlessly for the bliss and peace which none but you can provide.'

The females of every single species had found their way to him. Animals, birds, reptiles and aquatic creatures. Their furry bodies weaved their way through the throng, on entering his august presence they sheathed their claws, tucked their tails, put their fangs and forked tongues away. Gambolling, capering and writhing by his side, tears gave way to laughter at last. They had searched and finally found Kartikeya. Or he had found them. It made no difference.

Gathered in the bosom of feminine pulchritude, Kartikeya found his mind wandering where none dared follow, through the battlefield of his memories. He remembered the monotony of killing and his own complete lack of repugnance for the vicious vicissitudes of war. The air had been thick with missiles of death and destruction—lances, maces, clubs, flaming arrows, darts and daggers dripping with blood, spears and swords slick with suffering. They were an endless stream of offerings, libations to be poured over the flames of destruction so they could burn brighter, fed with blood.

Kartikeya remembered the celestial missiles that had been charged with the *tejas* of the Destroyer, concentrated in his own adamantine being that alone of all things in creation, besides the power of Shakti, could withstand its killing might. He remembered discharging it and the bloodlust that had flooded through him at the sight of those fleeing in all directions, their efforts entirely in vain as death closed in on them.

He felt the energy of Shiva coursing through him coupling with the wrath of Shakti, inflaming his senses as he claimed countless lives without pausing to draw breath, never pausing to question if so much death could indeed lead to the renewal of Dharma. But that was because he knew the answer. Chaos must be allowed to reign supreme if calm is ever to be restored.

Once again, he felt the irrepressible force build inside him and he welcomed its presence as he threw himself into the adoring masses and they all danced, laughed, cried, shouted and sang with joy.

There was no discipline in their ranks. Merely an overabundance of emotion. And Kartikeya was drenched in the powerful feelings they showered him with. Much had been taken from them. All that remained was devotion to the one who had done all the taking, leaving them hollowed out and empty, so they could be better filled with him alone. It made them melt with unalloyed desire that bubbled over and filled their hearts to the brim with ecstasy. Nothing they had lost had a tenth of the value of the one they had found or felt as sweet.

Seized with love, they surrendered shame and gathered around him as willing captives, secure in the knowledge that their hearts and souls were safe with him. Kartikeya gave generously, satiating their need for him. After everything they had gone through and the privations they had endured in the hopes that it would all lead to him, they deserved to have their desires fulfilled beyond their wildest imagining. So he took the hearts they insisted on giving to him for safekeeping and filled it with everything he had to give.

He belonged to them all. Each of the girls felt he belonged to her alone. They all believed it with every fibre of their being and their belief made it true. Kartikeya listened attentively to the one who wished to unburden her very soul. He held the other close to his chest because she needed him to make her feel safe and because she wanted nothing more than to melt into his arms, remaining in that haven for the rest of time.

He pampered her like no one had before and no one would again. He adored her every bit as much as she adored him because it was all she needed.

He fondled her in the way she loved for it was her pleasure that was his. He made love to her for aeons and made her forget every single hurt that had been done to her, reducing her very existence to an endless throbbing ecstasy. He cradled her in his arms till she fell asleep and allowed her cares to slip away, never to return.

None wanted to leave his side. They yearned for nothing while he was there. Each wanted to get as close to him as possible and remain that way forever. He belonged to them alone. Forgetting everything they had been and everything they ever wanted to be, they supped on contentment and spent eternity in that moment when he made everything better again.

All the girls had come to him looking for love and they had found it. The sun, moon and the stars alone bore witness to the play of their passion. Millions of bodies writhed in pairs, entwined so closely together as to resemble a single entity. Their bodily fluids were released in copious streams, merging together in a merry dance, forming rivulets that were diverted and divided before they soaked into the parched surface of Bhoomi Devi, burnt out by war and hate. Mother Earth thrived on a steady diet of all things sensuous and voluptuous, assuaging her appetite on seminal fluids that flowed in a never-ending stream, soaking her with the thrill of fulfilled longing and sated yearning. When the life-giving waters flowed into the dry soil, it was a match truly made in heaven.

Lands that lay fallow burst into life in a riot of bright colour, donning garments of lush green. Buds escaped their dark, subterranean prisons and broke through to the surface. Trees took root and rose high into the heavens, flirting with the clouds that kissed the tops of their swaying branches, glad to see them after so long. All around, life bloomed in joyous abandon.

Mother Earth was feeling expansive, having feasted on the hot juices of glorious desire and her gifts were so generous as to border on profligacy. Ripe fruits of every variety hung in bunches everywhere, ready to be picked and consumed. Golden grain grew in abundance, ready for the harvest. Vegetables rich in nutrients sprouted everywhere, ready to be consumed.

And still the unending sexual act went on uninterrupted, powered by a frenzy of love and lust.

It was the most scandalous thing and decent folks were appalled. The denizens of the three worlds looked askance at this uninhibited, vulgar, coarse display of runaway passion and shameless coupling. Horrified and boiling with outrage, they nevertheless could not avert their gaze.

So they looked on and on. Feelings of lechery and lasciviousness stirred in their own loins, lubricating repressed urges that hollered for satisfaction which wasn't coming. The men and women of all species who had been left out from the mass lovemaking felt the loss keenly. Like the pricking of needles that left no part of them untouched. They burned with unfulfilled desire. And anger.

Parvati's Unrest

ARVATI WAS NOT entirely pleased with the fruition of events
that she may or may not have had a hand in setting in motion.
What was it about the act of sexual congress that created such
a furore in the breasts of those who were engaged in it as well
as those who weren't? The infamous acts her son was engaging
in with everyone, irrespective of species, had been brought to
her notice by the more spiteful and self-appointed guardians of
morality belonging to both genders.

'You are not to blame at all for his peccadilloes,' the ones
who believed themselves to be well-meaning usually said,
which meant, of course, that they believed she had to bear
the brunt of the blame for her son's premature promiscuity,
'but it behoves you to put an end to this sort of licentious and
unseemly conduct that reflects poorly on his upbringing.'

'All males have urges which they have difficulty governing,
but even by such dubious standards, Kartikeya's actions are
deserving of censure. Why! Some of the creatures he lies with

have begrimed bodies, tentacles and hooked claws, not to mention faces that not even their own mother can look upon without revulsion.' These were the ones cursed with squeamish dispositions and overly sensitive sensibilities.

'They have befouled and polluted the three worlds with their unholy activities! Even Tarakasura seems like the epitome of restraint and decency by comparison.' Their concern for the environment and Bhoomi Devi would have been truly touching had it not been so hopelessly fake.

On and on they went on, till Parvati was heartily sick of it and sorely tempted to pluck the rod of self-righteousness wedged up their backsides and beat them all to death with it. Still, she wasn't too pleased with her son either, though she herself wasn't blinded by petty spite like the worst of his detractors.

The problem was that Kartikeya had a little too much of his father in him, though given the circumstances of his birth, that should not have surprised her as much as it did. Still it got her goat every single time when he displayed the same far from salubrious attributes that she liked least about Shiva.

Parvati loved Shiva. How could she not? But it was hard to like him let alone love him when he felt free to flaunt his infidelity with Ganga or when he abandoned his wife and repaired to the wild heights of Kailash with his Bhootaganas and Kali in tow, where they would have their fill of intoxicants and dance the hours away, before getting down to the serious business of endless intercourse. It was also why she blamed Shiva for Karti's sordid escapades and libido.

Parvati knew that there were times when Shiva chafed under the strictures enforced by matrimony and parenthood. She felt the same way too and it galled her that he did not realize or care that their union in many ways was even harder on her. He missed Shakti with an ardour that bordered on the manic but so did she. Being forced to take up the mantle of the auspicious woman who was expected to bear everything with a smile was not a role she relished. How would Shiva react, Parvati wondered, if she were to take a lover? Or two or three? Or even a hundred?

They still loved each other after a fashion. For that at least, Parvati was grateful. He still liked to visit her bed and cover her with his caresses. Even her smouldering anger and jealousy endeared her to the Destroyer. And yet she missed the early days, when their love had been so strong it had obliterated everything else. Now every time he touched her, she could not stop herself from bristling over remembered slights, still smarting grievances and a thousand feelings of resentment over the things he did or did not do. It was becoming harder and harder to forget his shortcomings enough to surrender herself entirely to him. Shiva meanwhile tended to view her recalcitrance as rejection and became increasingly injured.

When Kartikeya first came into their life, she had been wracked with grief and he had made it all better. But ultimately he had also made everything worse. Like his father before him, her handsome, special boy had broken her heart by losing his own to a dreaded enemy's daughter, daring to defy his mother in the matter of the trollop, then compounded his misdeed by making love to thousands of them. Shiva's son had made it painfully obvious that he too had loved her only to eventually leave her behind.

Cowardly as ever, in the face of her mounting unrest and anger, Shiva had taken to giving her a wide berth. Even when he was with her, he seemed distracted. As for Kartikeya, he was so busy with his loving companions, she doubted he knew or cared that his mother was still very much alive.

Shiva came to her then. It had been her intention to be warm and welcoming but unfortunately, the first words out her mouth sallied forth with a wanton will of their own, coated with the venom of her extreme irritation. 'Everybody seems to think your son is a disgrace and have been feeling perfectly free to give me an earful about his less savoury activities of late. It would be lovely if you could concern yourself with the issues plaguing your family for a change.'

'You look pretty when you are petulant,' he remarked with a leer which gadded her no end. 'Don't bother your head with the blithering of blustering buffoons. Besides, I thought you would be pleased at the temporary setback regarding his plan to unite himself with Indra's daughter at the earliest.'

Parvati ignored his levity. She had been meaning to ask him something for a while now and now was as good a time as any other. 'Don't you think it is high time we made ourselves another baby? Or do you think I am not worthy enough to bear your seed? It still bothers me that Indra's wiles interfered with the joyous culmination of our union.'

'Joyous culmination of our union?' He laughed at the words she had carefully chosen for the occasion after much deliberation. 'I like that we are still in the process of culminating our union. It does not sound so ominous nor as final as actual culmination at any rate, joyous or otherwise.'

He laughed at his own wit, till it became impossible to remain oblivious to his dear wife's mounting agitation. Shiva sighed softly, trying not to irk her, which only served to increase her ire to intolerable levels. 'Why do you want to have another child? Don't you have your hands full with this one? Or have you stopped thinking of him as your own? His love for another does not necessarily mean that his love for you has diminished in any way.'

Shiva gathered her in his arms, no doubt assuming that by mouthing inane platitudes and making love to her he would be able to kiss away the cares that beset her and restore the equanimity he liked best about his wife. After all this time, he still did not know her as well as she knew him. It was infuriating and made her want to hug him and hit him at the same time.

By the time he left her side, blissfully unaware or pretending to be unaware of her lack of enthusiasm for a formerly beloved sport that had lost much of its charm for her, Parvati's mind was completely and irrevocably made up. Though exhausted from their exertions and drenched in perspiration, hers and Shiva's both, which mingled sweetly together without the fuss and muss of their union, she gathered herself together for what needed to be done.

Slowly and with painstaking effort, she gathered together the natural oils of her body, mixing it with the drops of sweat and the cells which she had scraped off the surface, leaving deep, bloodied furrows on the hitherto, unblemished skin, not pausing till she had a lump of the stuff. It had been gathered from every part of her. She lavished attention on the child she was shaping, sparing no effort to make sure that everything was perfection, putting her heart and soul into it with all the love that was hers to offer.

Parvati poured the power of *prakriti* into the lovingly assembled parts of her, gathering together the strands of the infinite and weaving it into the finite, rendering the formless with graceful form, infusing into it the forces of creativity that were her own. Unbeknownst to the mother, much of her frustration with the men in her life as well as long repressed rage and pain flowed through her fingers as she worked, spreading itself over the flesh and bones of the being that emerged, lodging itself deep into the heart, therein transforming her weakness into strength. Then she breathed *prana* and *jiiva* into the unconscious body till it stirred with consciousness.

The child was exquisite, perfect in every imaginable way. And she was a beauty, like her mother. Her mother had named her Nesha. *You are the child of my very heart and all that I have that is entirely my own*, she thought, gazing fondly at her daughter, the beloved child of *prakriti*.

Parvati kept little Nesha by her side. Always. Her daughter was so tiny, fragile and impossibly lovely that she worried endlessly about baleful influences that may conspire to snatch away the happiness the baby had brought into her life yet again and she kept the little one close to her at all times. Parvati doted on her endlessly and nothing gave her more joy that bathing and feeding the baby, or rocking the precious little bundle to sleep in her arms while singing soothing lullabies to ward off the bad dreams.

While Nesha slept, she snuggled close to her, just to breathe in the scent of the baby and feel better about her own fears. And there were too many of them. The most overriding one, of course, being a deep and abiding concern for the new light of her life.

Karti had been part of a grand design, born to perform great deeds and the denizens of the three worlds remained in awe of him. Made in the image of the Destroyer, liberator of not just those who had been the victims of tyranny but the tyrants themselves, a proven warrior and lover, he was adored beyond all reason. Handsome and strong, it was impossible for everybody in the three worlds to not love him.

Even his harshest detractors who were vociferous in their condemnation of his recent libidinous pursuits could not resist admiring him in secret for the extreme potency and virility he displayed in the manner of his hyper masculine father. As was usually the case with these things, the women he lay with would be universally scorned while Karti would get away with a mild slap to the wrist and go back to being the beloved. There would never be a dearth of people to love him as dearly as she herself did, for as long as time ticked on.

Parvati couldn't help worrying about Nesha, though. She was being unreasonable and knew it, especially since her younger one was imbued with the raw power of Shakti and would no doubt wield it with ease. But still, the males in the divine pantheon seldom took kindly to feminine wielders of power, especially when it outstripped their own. Thinking about it filled her with unspeakable dread and Parvati swore that she would destroy the universe if anybody dared to even dream of hurting her daughter.

She had been apprehensive about Shiva's reaction to his daughter and her loving husband surpassed even her low expectations. He was awkward and uneasy around Nesha, behaving as though he were convinced the baby was going to bite. It made Parvati want to bite his head off.

Though Shiva wouldn't admit as much, it clearly bothered him that she had gone ahead and made this baby without his approval or help. Not that he had seen fit to consult her when he himself decided to interrupt their lovemaking to accede to the wishes of her enemy, Indra.

To make up for his reticence, Parvati lavished all her love

and attention on Nesha, devoting every moment of her time to the baby. Shiva had been mildly resentful at first but soon he was openly jealous. Secretly, it pleased Parvati to see him so envious and she saw no harm in stoking the flames just to get a rise out of him. Hadn't she suffered in silence all this time, unable to do a thing about her own jealousy regarding all who had boldly staked a claim on his affections emboldened by his own willingness?

In a foolish move to win the affection of his daughter, Shiva seemed to think it was appropriate to place a particularly fearsome serpent around her neck to amuse the baby but when the tyke felt the thing slither across her ribs, she had bawled in consternation, howling her outrage into his ears and making him jump in genuine fright.

'What?' he asked innocently when Parvati enfolded Nesha in a hug to calm her down, shooting the dirtiest look she could manage at her loving husband. 'Karti used to love playing with the snakes that adorn my person.'

She had let loose a stream of invective then which made Nesha scream some more. 'See what you have done?' she raged at Shiva, more upset than she could say that father and daughter seemed not to have warmed to each other instantly, which was all she had wanted. The new mother knew she was making things worse when she noticed Shiva looking hurt and sulking, but for some reason, she could not stop herself or govern her fears which were exacerbating an already precarious family situation.

Parvati wished Karti were with her. He would have loved his baby sister. How could he not? But then there were times when she doubted him too. After all, though he had claimed to love her best of all, he seemed to have difficulty extricating himself from the torrid embraces of his women in order to pay his new sister a visit.

Moreover, Parvati remembered the time Karti had remarked that he would prefer a bear to a sibling and given how like his father he was, he might just respond with jealousy. There were too many stories of sibling rivalry taking an ugly turn. Only recently someone had told her about the time Yama's daughter Madhu Swapna had accidently killed her brother Nidra, angered by the attention that was being showered upon him.

The horror story had made her shudder and she became even more protective about Nesha, refusing to let any of her attendants or Shiva's Ganas near her daughter. Suspicious of their intentions, she refused to entertain visitors and suffered even her husband's presence with ill-feeling.

'You love too excessively for yours or anybody else's good,' Shiva had shouted at her in exasperation. 'Nothing good can come of such an overblown feeling! What are you trying to prove? Nobody is going to hurt your little pet! You are alienating everybody by being so damnably ungracious! Even lionesses aren't this ferociously protective about their cubs!'

Parvati could not believe her ears. Had Shiva actually referred to their daughter as a pet? How dare he! 'Why don't you do me the kindness of taking yourself away from here? Your presence is odious to us. Leave me and my daughter alone and go play with your whores!'

Shiva face flushed with the force of his fury. The virulent blue of his throat darkened and the poison pushed against the calloused skin, 'Such disrespect on your part is a disgrace, Parvati! What is the matter with you? Why are you being such a...'

'You cannot talk to my mother like that!' Nesha came to her mother's defence at once, hurling her favourite rattle at Shiva.

'Tell that precocious child to stay out of this! She has no business coming in between a husband and wife!'

'Nesha has every right to be here! I am glad there is somebody to take my side every once in a while!'

Their fights became uglier and uglier, leaving them both battered and bruised. It reached a point where they were no longer on talking terms. The entire thing made her feel horrid and left her weeping bitter tears. It was Nesha who consoled her, 'Don't you cry, Mother! Nobody is worth so many tears. Besides things always get worse before they get better.'

She was right, of course. Parvati cheered up for her sake. Nesha was a joy to be with but she missed Shiva and Karti both, and she dreamed of the day when they would all be together. Nesha loved listening to stories about her heroic brother and pestered her endlessly for tales about his more extraordinary exploits. Parvati decided to leave out the salacious titbits about his amorous pursuits.

Having listened for the umpteenth time of Karti's exemplary services rendered to Bhoomi Devi that went above and beyond the call of duty, Nesha had dozed off, asleep in the crook of Parvati's arm. Fatigued, she had nodded off too. They woke up together, rudely interrupted from a deep slumber.

'It's my brother, Karti!' Nesha whispered. 'His grief is unbearable. He needs you, Mother. You must help him immediately before his heart breaks beyond repair!'

Afterburn After Afterglow

*T*HEY LAY IN silence, basking in the warm afterglow of love making, soaking in the ambience of supreme contentment and complete well-being. Everything was perfection. The air smelled sweet, all around them flowers bloomed and butterflies flitted around drunk on nectar, flirtatiously bestowing silken kisses. None of them had felt this complete or sated. It was a wonderful time to be alive.

Kartikeya seemed to be slumbering too. Except he wasn't. His thoughts were with Parvati and they made him mildly restive. He tried resisting thoughts of her, especially in light of the activities he had so recently engaged in. But the harder he tried, the more she loomed over his mind, putting everything else in the shadow of her presence.

After a while he gave up struggling. They were so finely attuned to each other's rhythms he could actually feel her unhappiness and it became his too. The raw expenditure of power, when she gave a part of herself to breathe life into another rocked his very being. He was overwhelmed and delighted as she was on the occasion of Nesha's birth. His heart contracted with love and he could barely wait to hold his little sister.

Parvati was right about him being his father's son too. Sure, he already loved little Nesha but if he were to be honest he would say that he was mildly annoyed at the thought that he would now have to share his parents with someone else. Besides he had been hoping that since Parvati had declared herself traumatized by his behaviour of late, she would be heartily sick of children.

In addition to that, he knew that his mother denied Shiva her bed when she was furious with him, and since that was more often than not these days, Karti had assumed he would be an only child. Now Shiva would be even less thrilled than he was at having been left out of the equation completely. And both of them would rationalize their feelings and insist on feeling more persecuted and ill-used by the other. Parents!

Their marital discord was bothering him a bit. He wished they would hurry up and get over their differences as soon as possible. It was awful when they were not getting along. He knew Parvati wanted him home, but there were a few things that he needed to take care of now that he had discharged his far from onerous duties to Bhoomi Devi.

Besides it was never a good idea for him to be in the vicinity when they were at each other's throats. Mother would take one look at him and decide that he reminded her of everything she detested about Shiva, while Father would seize the chance to curry favour with him by insisting that Parvati was being unfair to their only son, thereby triggering a flaming temper tantrum.

Kartikeya twirled a leaf lazily in his hand and wondered

if he and Devasena were also destined to spend an eternity bickering. Especially since there was another whom he hadn't ever seen or knew anything about and yet his heart reached out for her. He assured himself that things would be different with them and tried to turn a deaf ear to the voices in his head that were laughing uproariously at the little falsehoods he was feeding himself.

Indra kept his eye on Kartikeya from the heavens which had formerly been his domain, where he had lorded it over the three worlds, his supremacy unchallenged. It would always be that way, he had assumed, and saw no reason why he should not assert himself to make certain that things went back to the way they had been.

He summoned the storm clouds, filled to bursting with the full strength of their arsenal to shield him and conceal his advance, as he drew stealthily closer to his quarry. Kartikeya was stretched out luxuriously on a bed of bodies that extended as far as the eye could see. Indra paused to take a closer look at him. Every aspect of Shiva's son was annoyingly perfect. He hated that about him. That, and the fact that he seemed to inspire nothing but love in the hearts of everyone. It was most infuriating and the reason his idiotic brothers had seen fit to beg him to become their King, never mind that their rightful leader who had kept them safe from the malice of the Asuras was still very much alive.

The Wielder of the Thunderbolt took in the sight of the quiescent bodies that lay coiled all over the place, worn out no doubt from an excessive indulgence in copulation. Indra found he was revolted but fully aroused as well. Sachi was more objective about these things and she had declared that Kartikeya's actions were beyond reprehensible.

'Shiva's son is a voluptuary; make no mistake about it, and a particularly vile one!' she had insisted. 'He burns with a rapacious fire and many are the fools who are fatally drawn to his irresistible power and magnetism. Have you seen how he looks at his victims? There is something in that piercing gaze at once noble yet crafty. He makes them his captives who are more than willing to do anything he asks, no matter how indecent.

'Those with a shred of honour flee from his unwanted advances. But he is insatiable and will not stop till he has had them all. Can't you hear their cries for help? Their heart-rending pleas to be spared from his hateful manhandling, brutal violation of their bodies and their enslavement. It is nothing less than your duty to rid the three worlds of this menace.'

Indra decided she was right as he skulked in the shadows. It was his duty to rid the three worlds of this boy, who had become the monster he had been created to destroy. He ignored the cautionary voice that observed that his so-called victims certainly weren't complaining about his unseemly behaviour.

Still, Indra could have forgiven Shiva's son for a dozen perversions but he would be damned before allowing the little rapscallion to establish his sovereignty over the three worlds. This is what he got for appealing to the ever contrary Destroyer for his help. Somehow, he had a knack for throwing things out of whack, irrespective of whether he was immersed in the fires of *tapas* or submerged in conjugal bliss.

Why couldn't he be more like Vishnu, who simply got rid of pesky claimants to the throne of heaven before making a gracious exit? Shiva, on the other hand, who had long expressed disdain for the trappings of power, seemed keen on foisting his brat on them to the detriment of Indra's grand ambition. For a brief moment, Indra hesitated. He was contemplating acting against Mahadeva's son, the one they referred to as Mahasena, who had chased away Maya's beastly brood as if they had been little more than irksome insects. It was tantamount to suicide. Or worse.

Indra forced such counterproductive contemplation from his head. In fact, he banished all thoughts from his conscious mind, deciding that endless analysis was akin to paralysis. It was time to seize the moment and do the needful to restore himself to his former glory and splendour. He had done it before in the past—destroying his enemies mercilessly without a thought or a great deal of cold calculation to take back what was his by right.

The attack was sudden and seemed to come at the sleeping forms from everywhere. Storm clouds unloosed their burdens and pelted them with a deadly rain that could kill, with its poisoned droplets landing everywhere with the force of plummeting rocks. Bolts of lightning tore into the ranks of those who had nothing to defend themselves with.

Thousands took to their heels only to be mowed down by the merciless rain, which burnt through the cover offered by the dense, broad canopy of the tress. To the accompaniment of the sombre timbre of thunder, the *Vajra*, deadliest of Indra's missiles, conjured up a terrifying tempest and a hailstorm of destruction that rocked Mother Earth to her very foundation.

Gale winds tore up trees by the roots, howling their battle cry as they decimated entire forests without the slightest trace, toppling all dwellings, destroying the harvest, killing the fishes, birds, beasts and seeking to blow all of creation asunder. Indra expended all his power into the *Vajra*, keeping it up for days on end, determined to take no chances were Shiva's son was concerned. It had been too easy and that bothered him above all else.

Indra kept the invincible *Vajra* in play, not daring to call it back till he could be certain of Kartikeya's demise. He shut his ears to the dying wails of the many who, despite their lacerated lungs and tattered tongues, dredged up the strength to curse him with their last breath.

'May your transgressions catch up with you, leaving you to die!'

'May Lord Kartikeya's messengers carry the news of your death to the she-devil who spawned you and every one of the countless demons who had a hand in siring the likes of you!'

'You will die in pain, alone and unwanted, coughing up blood and leaking foul pus from every one of the unsightly vulvas on your accursed body!'

Indra paid the insults no heed, though he wished people would refrain from casting slurs on his sainted mother for every one of his admittedly numerous faults. He did not stop till the *Vajra* tore through all the participants of the act, until nothing remained of them, not even droplets of blood or even the dust they had been ground into.

Incredibly, Kartikeya seemed to have slumbered through it all even as the *Vajra* raised all manner of hell around him, and sat up lazily when all his partners in copulation had been obliterated into oblivion. He was still rubbing his eyes lazily when the thunderbolt took him high in the chest, plunging deep into his heart, tearing it apart. It was the most satisfying kill Indra had ever experienced and it felt better than the most intense of emotions. The brute force of the invincible *Vajra* saw his perfect form split in three, mangling parts of those perfectly sculpted contours, making a mockery of his former handsomeness.

It was something of a travesty, Indra had to concede with a pang of pity, but the brutality of his pitiful death was also somehow fitting for the murderer who had claimed three lives and nearly destroyed the three worlds with his army of barbarian brutes even before he grew to full manhood. Still, he'd had a lot of potential and it was a pity.

Bhoomi Devi was already mourning the loss of a beloved son who had filled her so recently with his potency, rendering her fecund. Discarding her preferred brightly coloured garments, she donned sackcloth and ashes, weeping copious tears that were not sufficient to put out the fires of the *Vajra*.

It had been too easy though. Killing Kartikeya had been simply a matter of taking him unawares. The niggling doubts wouldn't go away, robbing him of the sublime satisfaction of the moment. 'For better or for worse, the deed is done,' he said aloud, to reassure himself, turning around for one last look at his handiwork.

Indra stared in stunned disbelief as the dust settled to reveal the sylvan surroundings that had been the chosen venue of Kartikeya for his games of love. The locale was serenely beautiful and did not show the slightest sign of its fatal encounter with the *Vajra*. Kartikeya's lovers had woken up, though. They were glaring at him, infuriated that he had put an end to their pleasure party. Shooting him dirty looks fit to curdle the divine nectar of immortality, they embraced Kartikeya in turns and melted away into his person.

A gentle breeze sprang up and a cloudless sky shorn of storm clouds looked down benevolently upon that tranquil setting. Bhoomi Devi preened, her beauty in full bloom, bestowing all her love upon the creatures that gambolled about her person. Everything was alive and thriving. Indra alone felt the cold and clammy hand of fear, heralding the approach of certain death. He smiled morosely. Even at a time like this, he derived a measure of happiness from having been right all along. It had been too easy to be true.

Kartikeya sat alone at the very epicentre of the clearing, looking at him with those brilliant eyes that Sachi had described so vividly. He stood transfixed before that gaze, rendered helpless as a new-born babe, unable to withstand the scrutiny that had stripped him bare of all secrets.

'It is impossible!' Indra said, finding his voice at last, though it sounded slightly shrill. 'I saw it with my own eyes. None can withstand the might of my *Vajra*. Your whores were reduced to the dirt that had spawned them and you yourself were ripped into three different pieces.'

'You are right,' Kartikeya nodded. 'It was certainly what you intended for me, at any rate. I find it somewhat mean, in addition to being unacceptably ungrateful.'

Indra blinked. Once again he saw the broken remains of Shiva's son. But they were not leaking his red blood; instead, smoky tendrils spilled out lazily from the gaping wounds he had sustained. The shadowy apparitions were coalescing into weird, deformed creatures who gathered themselves and came at him in a rush.

He refused to give ground, though they circled around him hissing and snarling, toying with their prey instead of giving him the relief of a quick end. Was this the damned compassion Kartikeya was supposedly famed for?

'Who are these fiendish creatures?' he called out to Kartikeya, defiant unto death and whatever came beyond.

Shiva's son stood whole, unharmed, looking even better than Indra recalled.

'You will have to do better than these freaks to be rid of me,' the Wielder of the Thunderbolt shouted, through clenched teeth.

Kartikeya did not reply. He merely watched as his pets closed in on Indra, obscuring him entirely, snapping and clawing at each other in their frenzy to get at him.

The golden-hued spirits that had spilled out from his mauled right side reached him first. They were horrible to look upon, demoniacal in their demeanour, glaring at him with red eyes that rolled about wildly in their sockets, dizzy with implacable hatred.

'We are the Grahas,' they rasped in his ears, with voices so shrill they caused blood to pour out from every aperture, which they licked with rough tongues. 'You are a fool for thinking you can hurt those of us who have given entirely of ourselves to Lord Kartikeya! Didn't you know that he will always protect us from the likes of you? Foolishness such as yours is an unforgiveable crime. Are you ready for the punishment you so richly deserve?'

They tore off strips of his flesh and tossed it to their sister spirit creatures who reached out eagerly, devouring entire chunks of Indra in minutes. They were even more repellent than the Grahas, broad of shoulders, hirsute, long-toothed, cursed with foul breath, smeared all over with dirt, ash and everything abhorrent. 'We are the Matrikas, daughters of divine wrath and we come bearing the gift of vengeance. Our fealty is to the divine Kartikeya. Flesh and blood are the victuals we dine on, and yours will make for a hearty repast. The denizens of the three worlds will thank us for digesting your odious remains.'

Bleeding from his many wounds, considerably weakened and reduced to the truly lamentable state of witnessing the most hideous beings in existence feasting on his viscera, Indra summoned the last of his flagging strength to hurl his thunderbolt into their midst, scattering them in all directions. But they regrouped almost immediately, laughing raucously at his sudden display of bravery.

The warrior women emerged from their ranks moving in for the kill. Armed to the teeth and more powerfully built than the worst of his antagonists from among the Asuras, they had swords and lances for limbs, and were bristled with the glint of battle lust in their protuberant, bulging eyes. 'We are the Kumaris, Lord Kartikeya's lovers and fighters. We are the stalkers of evil and we will pursue the perpetrators to the ends of the universe to make them pay for their heinous crimes.'

They were as good as their word, hacking at him, forcing him to his knees. But he would not repent before carrion beasts such as them who lived on offal. 'Whores! You can kill me over and over again till your bloodlust is satiated but mark my words, you will not succeed in destroying the true King of the three worlds and the mighty Wielder of the Thunderbolt.'

The Grahas, Matrikas and Kumaris laughed long and hard at his passionate proclamation, chewing on his severed limbs and swallowing great gobs of his flesh as they smacked their putrescent lips with ghoulish relish.

Indra could not feel his soul being ripped free from his body. 'Mark my words! There will be a day of reckoning for the horrors that have transpired on this day. I will prevail as will every infinitesimal atom that was formerly a part of me. They will endure in the life-giving fluids of the womb of virtuous women and I will avenge the humiliation, I was unfairly subjected to.'

Their voices were harsh with the force of their mounting anger. 'You will not escape us, duplicitous creature, guilty of the foulest of deeds. We will follow you and others afflicted with the same propensity for evil into the wombs you seek to pollute, scouring it clean of your malicious intent. We will burn out the taint by striking down mothers infected by vicious villains, freeing them as well as their babies from baleful influences that would have otherwise reduced their lot to one of endless suffering.'

'Do your worst!' Indra howled. 'I will never ever surrender. You will rue the day you crossed me forever more.' His last words of anguish were torn out at the same time as his last breath, and he addressed them directly to Kartikeya, 'You are not quite as clever as you think you are. The cruelty you have subjected me to will eventually rebound on you! Even Shiva will not be able to protect you from the consequences of your fallen deeds.'

'I don't expect him to!' Kartikeya told him with a strange, sad smile. 'As for you, we will meet again on the other side of the admittedly unpleasant journey you have chosen to embark on.'

The Grahas, Matrikas and Kumaris struggled to make a complete end of him, determined to make sure that not a trace remained of Indra, the mighty Wielder of the Thunderbolt. But he was obstinate and as good as his word. Infinitesimal pieces of him defied their attempts to capture them, and disappeared into the distance, scattering in all directions and spreading far and wide. With wild cries of outrage, the fiercest of adversaries chased after them, till they too were reduced to specks in the distance.

Backlash, Agony and Ecstacy

IT HAD NOT been the most pleasant of experiences and had left him feeling hollowed out. These intense encounters were a little too heavy for Kartikeya's tastes and he finally understood why Shiva liked to traipse off into the wilderness and detach himself entirely from everything, leaving the three worlds to get by on their own. He promised himself that he would do the same thing someday.

Chitra materialized by his side. Kartikeya had never seen his unflappable mount this agitated or so dangerously close to tears. 'What's wrong?' he asked, his instincts warning him that it was the worst of tidings. For a moment, he wished Chitra wouldn't tell him.

Carried thither by his peacock, Kartikeya could make out all that remained of her, which was next to nothing, like the memory of a sweet fragrance. Yet, Devasena's gentle presence suffused every part of the little hut where she had chosen to make her home, away from him and her father both. The blooms she had raised with her own hand stood wilting on bent stalks, mourning the loss of the loving hands that had cared for them. The woodland creatures she had befriended lamented her passing with plaintive cries that tore at his heart far more painfully than her father's *Vajra* had managed.

All the things she had touched and used lay intact, no doubt assuming their owner would use them again and it seemed inconceivable that she would never again do so. Kartikeya had trouble processing how any of this was possible. 'We are meant to be with each other,' Devasena had said, and he had known beyond a shadow of a doubt that it was so. How then had it come to pass that she was gone and he remained?

'I don't understand,' Chitra said the words so softly, Kartikeya barely heard him. It was another first. He did not reply and it wasn't only because he did not understand himself. He didn't wish to either.

So he listened dully as Chitra went on, trying to make sense of it. 'I was searching for the Princess as you had sent me to do. But it was notoriously difficult and I could not help thinking that something or someone was deliberately obstructing the way...' He hesitated to give voice to his suspicions but Karti heard them anyway.

Chitra waited for his response but when it wasn't forthcoming, he ploughed ahead with his narrative, needing to get it all out, 'But they found her first. I tried in vain to stop them. They were the same Shaktis Indra inadvertently released when he foolishly sought to skewer you in three.'

The great bird lowered himself and lay at his feet. Kartikeya stroked the graceful arch of his neck, as he relived the horrific things that had taken place before his very eyes. 'Why would they attack her? What harm has she ever done anyone? The strange thing was she seemed to be expecting them and was so accepting of her fate that I could barely stand it. You have to believe me, there was nothing I could do. There were too many of them. But I told them that Devasena had your love and they should not dare harm her, unless they wished to incur your wrath. They refused to listen, insisting that they were beholden to you and were merely doing what needed to be done. She carried the taint of your enemy in her blood, they said, and that part of her would never forgive you for what was done to Indra.'

Kartikeya continue to pat poor Chitra who was distraught. 'I went to her in the end and offered to carry her away to you, but she said that there was no need. The Princess made me promise to take care of you. She insisted that it would be best if you did not blame anybody for what happened to her and to assure you that it was only a matter of time before she found her way back to your side, which is where she truly belongs. It would be sooner than you might think, she added.'

Time slowed to a crawl. During the long days that followed, Chitra never left his side. Karti clung to the last words she had uttered like a lifeline, while he was tossed about mercilessly in a sea of grief. It felt like he had waited forever, every moment passing with agonizing slowness, but she had not come back to him. Perhaps he should follow his father's footsteps and immerse himself in the cleansing fire of *tapas*. But he had neither the will nor the inclination for it.

He remained in her home among her things, convinced that if he refused to let go, she couldn't possibly go. The question though, was why had he let her go in the first place? And having let her go why hadn't he lost no time in finding her immediately? If they were truly meant for each other, shouldn't it have been as simple as inevitably finding each other and staying together forever? Why did these things have to get so complicated? What purpose did all the drama serve? Was any of it worth anything in the long run?

There were moments when he was fully convinced that nothing mattered. Not even his own profound grief, or who got to rule the three worlds, or any of it. His debilitating pain dissipated slowly but surely, though he held onto it for all it was worth. The precious memories of their time together grew increasingly hazy. And still he held on to the remnants of his fading recollection of her essence, refusing to let go, even when it seemed that he must.

He kept up his ruminations, even if they felt pointless as well. Kartikeya was getting sick of himself and Chitra's devotion, especially since the peacock had regained his good equilibrium and seemed to take a more prosaic view of an epic love story that had barely taken root before being plucked out.

'You cannot be prostrate with grief forever,' he assured him sagely, 'nor live with a ghost gleaned from the echoes of a faded past. The future beckons to you with open arms and it behoves you to return the embrace. There is much that is left for you to experience rich in flavour as well as fulfilment, believe me.' Kartikeya supposed he was right and admitted to himself that he could hardly wait for this awful phase in his existence to get over as quickly as possible.

When Shiva paid him a visit, Kartikeya was far more pleased than he was willing to admit. His father sat next to him in companionable silence, an unobtrusive and reassuring presence. The snakes that had been his childhood companions crawled over his limbs, expressing their commiseration. For some reason, Shiva seemed to derive a lot of satisfaction from the comfortable rapport he shared with some of his more gruesome accoutrements.

'Are you still fighting with Mother?' he asked Shiva.

'I most certainly am not,' came the response, 'but she insists on fighting with me all the time. It is most unreasonable of Parvati.'

Kartikeya snorted in exasperation. 'Is that why you are being mean to Nesha as well?'

'What is a Nesha?' Shiva enquired, prompting his son to punch him on his arm. 'That does not hurt in the slightest, but you get your violent tendencies from Parvati. As for her new obsession, it is worse than the ones that preceded it. Besides she can't possibly expect anything good to come off defying my authority.'

'Your authority?' Karti rolled his eyes at him. 'If you could only listen to yourself you would be able to appreciate how ludicrous that sounded. After all, it was you who told me that you are little more than a corpse without her. I wish the two of you would go back to being in love. That would be nauseating in the extreme but anything is preferable to this discord. Besides, the smart ones among us know enough to appreciate the good things we have before it is taken away from our grasp.'

Shiva put an arm around him, 'Believe me, this too shall pass. And don't you worry about your mother and I, Karti. Despite what you think, we are not entirely hopeless. Besides, I'd rather talk about you than the constant source of joy that my marriage is.'

Karti shrugged, 'I know only one thing. Devasena will be returned to me soon, simply because I have no intention of spending aeons engaged in the performance of penances while waiting for her to take birth again. Why people turn their backs on life only to overindulge at a later stage I'll never know and don't intend to find out.'

He waited for his father to lecture him about his recalcitrance and foolhardiness. Instead Shiva clapped him on the shoulders in warm approbation. 'It is good that your mind is irrevocably made up. Now all you have to do is whatever it takes to fulfil its dictates. You may take after me, as your mother keeps reminding both of us, but you are not me and that is entirely for the best.'

And with those words he was gone. His visit had done Kartikeya a world of good. Kartikeya sat up straight, and told Chitra to make himself scarce. The noisome bird had wanted to know everything he had discussed with Shiva, though they both knew he had been shamelessly trying to eavesdrop and stopped himself from getting within hearing distance, simply because he had a healthy fear and respect for Shiva's third eye.

When he was sure that he was alone, Karti decided it was finally time for a certain difficult journey he had been putting off for a long time now—reach out to Parvati and ask, nay, beg for her help. His mother responded instantly, almost as if she had spent all the time they had been apart waiting for him. Kartikeya was gratified. He *had* been right about being her favourite, and it pleased him no end that nothing had changed even after little Nesha had arrived in their lives.

You have not been taking good care of yourself. Why, you are little more than skin and bones. Come home to me and let me fatten you up. Besides, don't you think it is about time you showed a little courtesy and thoughtfulness by honouring your sister with a visit? Her voice sounded disembodied and there was warmth and frost both in her tone. It was by far the nicest thing he had heard in a long time.

'Nesha is a credit to you, Mother,' he told her seriously, 'and I think she understands that ever since she came into our lives, I have loved her with all my heart and will always do so.'

Words are wind... Parvati groused, but he knew that she was pleased. *I am told Shiva paid you a visit. He likes having a sympathetic ear to pour out his grievances, especially where I am concerned.*

Kartikeya shook his head, refusing to bite, 'I know better than to take sides where the two of you are concerned. In fact, this is the very first lesson I am going to impart to Nesha. Are you sure it is a good idea to turn the baby against her own father?'

Don't you dare presume to know more than your mother! You are afflicted with Shiva's ego and it blinds you to the truth!

Her voice was a whiplash and he winced. 'Mother, it is not my place to give you unsolicited counsel. Besides, I only wished to ask that you grant my request.'

He felt her draw back at once. *Even I cannot spare you from the whim of fate nor inure you from the pain of parting.*

At least she had not refused him outright. It emboldened him to persist, 'Give her back to me, Mother! Even if it is the worst thing in the world for Devasena and me to be together. Even if all the ill-will Indra bears the two of us is contained within her. It does not matter even if you have foreseen that our union will end in unspeakable tragedy. That the love we bear each other may someday turn sour and we may just turn on each other with loathing, all the more unendurable because of the love that preceded it. None of it is adequate reason for us to be apart.

'Greatest of the Goddesses! Give her back to me! So what if a part of her could never forgive me for what has happened? It is perfectly reasonable given what I have done to her father. Nobody in their right mind would hold it against her. And so what if she wishes to avenge Indra and kill me? It is something for the two of us to deal with. Nobody has the right to interfere. Not even you, Mother.

'I understand that you are scared for me but even if your worst fears regarding Devasena were to be realized someday, I would still choose to be with her despite being fully aware of my fate. The happiness I know that I will find in her arms, even if it is achingly ephemeral, will make everything else bearable! Please, Mother! Please! Restore her to me!'

His impassioned outburst was met with a long silence that seemed to stretch on forever. Karti had expected as much. 'Take all the time you need to think about it and be as difficult as you please but we both know that you cannot deny me anything!'

Like your father, you too are taking advantage of my good heart and benevolent disposition. Will you persist in this folly? Remember that Indra's daughter will never be welcome in my home and neither will you if you choose her over your family.

'I will no more choose her over my family than I would choose Father over you. You don't need me to tell you that.'

Words are wind…but very well, seeing that I cannot dissuade you from this foolishness, you shall have what your heart desires. May you never regret your decision, though I do regret it already.

And that was that, Kartikeya hoped. He fell back exhausted. It felt good to fall asleep with the certain knowledge that when he awoke it would all be much better. This was something he knew for certain because the last thing he heard before sleep claimed him was a little girl's voice. *Mother is crying. But they are her happy tears because you returned to her. I hope you and Devasena will be very happy together. Don't forget to come and see me, brother!*

'I won't!' he replied.

Almost But Not Quite

$\mathcal{K}$ARTIKEYA AND HIS consort were out for a walk. Chitra felt he had to accompany them in his self-appointed role as their Protector and since Devasena thought he was adorable, it was agreed that he could come along provided he kept his beak shut and maintained a respectful distance. The peacock did as he was told, looking very injured indeed.

Still, he did keep me sane till I could be reunited with Devasena, Karti could not help thinking fondly. Things had been more than a little intense with Devasena returned to them from the dead. It had taken a little while for her to convince Chitra that she was not an avenging spirit still reeking with the rot of the grave. Devasena could not explain it herself. One moment she was dead, the next she was alive.

'It had felt like a really long nap,' she told them both, 'where you get the feeling that you are free falling through space and kick out wildly in a blind panic except I did not wake up. Then I got used to it and there were bouts of exhilaration and alarm both. Just at the point where I was convinced that the landing upon which I was to smash and break into a million pieces was close, I felt something yanking me back. The next thing I knew, it was time to live again. It is good to be back with you both.'

Impulsively, she had hugged them both. Karti swung her around in wild circles till she could no longer walk straight. They had all cried a little and laughed a lot. Time passed by in a golden haze of euphoria. The lovers enjoyed each other's company immensely, feeling like old friends who could talk about anything. Making up for lost time, they spent every moment together, as close as two peas in a pod, with Chitra squeezing himself in as well. Devasena tended to be indulgent with him, but Karti was stricter, which had led to Chitra deciding that he liked her better.

'He wasn't always this way, you know,' she began, lacing her fingers through his in a familiar gesture which he loved. 'When Jayanta and I were children, we always felt that our family was the best in the three worlds. My father was the grand sovereign of the three worlds and his time was hardly his own. Those seeking his favour were more numerous than the grains of sand or stars in the sky and they would throng to Amaravati, refusing to leave without an audience with him and there were all the prayers addressed to the Thunder God to be answered.'

Devasena seemed lost in her selective memories of her father and Karti saw no reason to burst her bubble, choosing to listen in silence as she shared her thoughts with him. Still, as far as he knew, Indra was nowhere as unselfish as she seemed to believe and had preferred to delegate tedious chores to his underlings while relaxing from the pressures of Kingship with a bevy of beautiful Apsaras.

'When he did manage to get away for a few moments with Jayanta and me, it was pure magic!' Devasena was saying. 'We once told him that it would be good fun to sail across the heavens in Surya's chariot and he immediately summoned the Sun God, overruling his vociferous protests, before elbowing him aside, bundling us inside and taking the reins himself! What a ride that was! Surya was near apoplectic with rage at this usurpation of his power but Father just laughed. I found out later that even Surya's own children had been denied this great honour. How proud and privileged Jayanta and I felt!

'Mother used to be jealous because we lived for each and every one of father's infrequent visits. He would always make up for it by bringing us wondrous gifts and dazzling us with outrageous stories involving heroes, demons and magic. We both treasured every single moment with him.'

Her eyes were sparkling and despite himself, Kartikeya was deeply moved. Indra could not have been too bad, at least in the beginning. Karti wondered exactly what affliction had eaten away his brain to the point where he saw fit to lock his daughter up in a cage to be used as bait and tried to murder Kartikeya, though he himself had expended a lot of time and energy in addition to sacrificing the life of Kamadeva to bring him into being.

'There were many among the Asuras who sought to hurt him by coming after either Jayanta or me,' Devasena shut her eyes, awash in memories. 'The worst was a monster named Keshin who once kidnapped me, after brutally murdering my personal guard. Even now I can barely stand the thought that they gave up their lives for my sake. My skin still crawls when I remember how roughly that fiend treated me. Father found us and his dear face was the most beautiful sight in the three worlds, though it was dark with fury! He beat up that detestable villain to within an inch of his life, cut off the hand that had dared manhandle his daughter and left him to bleed to death. We rode away together with his screams of agony ringing in our ears.

'Then he grabbed me by the shoulder, looked deep into my ears and told me something that I still carry in my heart—*You are Indra's daughter, don't you ever forget that. Don't you dare let anybody scare you into submission!* When I defied him years later, I could have sworn that he was proud of me. He left me in the cage, knowing that you would find me...'

Kartikeya felt bad for her. Terrible tragedy had overcome her family and there was much that was lost to her for good. Indra had lost his throne and kingdom to Maya's son, his beloved son and heir had been tortured and murdered by Taraka, he himself had come to grief, and his Queen Sachi had immolated herself on learning of her husband's disgrace and demise. Devasena also had died for her father's sins.

She smiled at him, 'Don't feel too bad for me. I have you, and that is more than enough. However, it grieves me deeply that you are practically estranged from your own mother on my account. It is not right. You must go to her at once. She needs you. As does you little sister. She is a baby and simply cannot handle the rift between your parents.'

Kartikeya sighed and said, 'I cannot leave you. Losing you is a risk I simply cannot take.' He did not think it necessary to tell her that Parvati had issued orders preventing the entry of Devasena into Kailash. How could he visit his mother when she insisted on treating his chosen wife so shabbily? He missed Parvati too but he saw no way around the stalemate that did not involve dishonouring Devasena.

'You won't lose me,' she promised, 'and I can take care of myself. I am Kartikeya's wife, am I not? Besides, Chitra told me the real reason for your hesitation. Don't frown at him like that; I extracted the information though he protested with all his might.'

Devasena laughed when he rolled his eyes at her and Chitra both. 'Eventually your mother will come around to accepting me. We'll make it work, you'll see. In the meantime, don't allow the rift with Goddess Parvati to widen. She has not forbidden entry to you, and if I were you, I would count my blessings and make haste to see her without testing her forbearance.'

'Oh! Mother cannot stay angry with me and she will forgive me anything.'

'That may be the case,' Devasena said as diplomatically as she could manage, 'but the truth is, a mother's hatred of her daughter-in-law has been known on occasion to outweigh her love for her dear son.'

'Those aren't your words,' he said, and without warning hurled his *vel* at Chitra, who howled in protest, feigning injured innocence. Devasena laughed so hard at their antics they forgot to stay annoyed with each other.

Not long after that, Kartikeya and Chitra found themselves headed towards home, urged thither by Devasena's repeated prodding, which Chitra warned him was dangerously close to nagging. 'You are well on your way to becoming an ignominious henpecked husband. But I should thank you for teaching me to treasure my independence and convincing me that marriage is not for birds.'

'The fact that you are too in love with your own self

to share yourself with another has nothing to do with your decision to remain single? Or that no self-respecting peahen will have any truck with you.'

'They are all too threatened by my good looks!' came the rejoinder. 'You are lucky you don't have the same problem.'

It felt good to return to the icy heights of Kailash, warmed only by the presence of his parents, though by all accounts their fighting had exacerbated to the point where the chill between them was a palpable thing.

Surprisingly, Chitra declined to accompany him to his mother's abode, insisting that he saw a murderous glint in Parvati's eyes whenever they rested on him, and there was absolutely no reason to risk his neck. He remained adamant when Kartikeya told him he was just being fanciful since, as far as he knew, Parvati did not care enough about him to kill him where he stood. Chitra however was unmoved.

With a shrug, he had carried on. His heart filled to the brim with love and pleasant anticipation at the thought of seeing Parvati again. Suddenly his path was barred by a fierce little girl armed with a gleaming staff. With a pang, he realized that Parvati had given it to her. She was a charming creature with flashing eyes and a wondrous head of curls. Chitra would have described her as the female version of Kartikeya himself.

'I cannot let you enter!' her voice rang with boldness and authority. 'My mother is indisposed and said that she will not see anybody today.'

Kartikeya felt the anger uncoil itself from deep within him. Nobody had dared to address him in such disrespectful tones or been so utterly unafraid of the Destroyer's power that was concentrated in him. He took a moment to suppress the sudden urge to hurl his *vel* at her bared chest.

'I think she will see me, mighty warrior! Especially since I am her favourite child and always will be!'

Nesha's warlike expression changed in a trice to one of surprised delight. Dropping her staff which landed heavily on his feet, she launched herself into his arms. 'It is you!' she shrieked into his ear so loudly he forgot all about his throbbing limb. 'Mother told me you were the bravest and noblest boy in the three worlds! And you are even more handsome than I imagined you would be. As for being Mother's favourite, I am not the one she has refused to see.'

Kartikeya hugged her back. 'Did she really say she will not see me?'

Nesha sounded apologetic, 'Her exact words were, "I will not be disturbed! Not by Shiva nor his son who saw fit to abandon his mother and run away with her enemy's daughter."'

Kartikeya looked so unabashedly crestfallen that Nesha felt sorry for him. 'Don't worry, she doesn't hate you as much as that mean husband of hers, who makes her cry all the time. Not a day goes by without her talking or thinking about you.'

Karti felt a rush of affection and annoyance towards Nesha. Conflicting emotions must be his inheritance from his parents. The two of them sat on the steps on the threshold and Kartikeya gave Nesha the gift basket Devasena had painstakingly put together for her. She loved the sweetmeats, though he could tell that she was mildly irritated with the talking dolls and magical toys his consort had insisted she would love. Kartikeya gave her the bow he had carved himself and an inexhaustible quiver of arrows which had been gifted to him by Varuna. Nesha squealed so loudly, Kartikeya's ears throbbed in protest. Still, there was something about the child that it made it impossible not to love her, even when she had positioned herself like a rock between him and Parvati.

'Mother is wrong about one thing though; you are nothing at all like Shiva.' Nesha was clearly not one to mince words and it was painfully apparent that she intended it as a compliment.

'Once you get to know our father a little better, you will feel differently,' Karti told her seriously. 'They call him Mahadeva for a reason. He is the greatest of the Gods and I worship the ground he walks on and always will. When Mother stops being angry at him, she will be happy to tell you the same.'

Nesha did not seem too convinced. 'But he is so mean to her and makes her cry all the time. When she is hurting from his words or actions, he does not bother to comfort or console her. Instead he behaves as though she alone is to blame for her unhappiness. Remember that golden deer grandfather gave her on the occasion of their marriage? Well, there was this one time when their argument grew spectacularly ugly and he reduced the poor thing to a smouldering pile of ash.'

Karti closed his eyes in distress. Parvati would have been inconsolable. She had loved that stupid deer though he himself had found it a tad insufferable, especially since he preened a lot more than even Chitra. What had Shiva been thinking? And since when did his mother start allowing little girls to fight her battles? But that was the problem; neither of them seemed to be doing a whole lot of thinking, both clearly determined to be the rock to the other's hard place.

Nesha was looking at him intently. Karti scooped her up and placed her on his lap. 'Listen, little one! I don't think you should take sides where our parents are concerned. It will be difficult but we have to remain neutral, if there is to any hope at all of our family weathering their marital storm and emerging relatively unscathed.'

She shook her head so violently, her curls got entangled with his. 'How can you say that? I refuse to stand aside and watch while he treats my mother so callously.'

'Our mother and his wife,' Karti pointed out. 'Like it or not, he has first claim on her affection. And whatever problems they are going through right now, they will sort it out eventually but not before putting each other through hell first. Mother is also guilty of having hurt him more often than either would care to remember, though she favours a far more subtle approach when it comes to the infliction of pain.'

'I was told that you are partial to your father…'

'Our father!' Karti corrected her.

She nodded irritably, before continuing, 'As I was saying, husband or not, Shiva does not have the right to treat her the way he does and I will never stand for it. I whacked him with my staff when he burnt her golden deer and do you know what he did? He sent his Ganas to teach me a lesson but I bashed their loutish heads in and sent them packing. You should have seen them run! Mother said it served them right.'

Karti was not at all happy to hear how much things continued to deteriorate between his mother and father. He hated that already there had been too many casualties but he supposed it was inevitable, if not right, with both of them on the warpath. Still not many faced the wrath of Shiva's Ganas, single-handedly no less, and lived to tell the tale. He supposed he was a little impressed and may even bring himself to admit that Parvati had outdone herself with this one. He mussed Nesha's hair affectionately and she smiled warmly at him, without the slightest hint of guile.

'I myself am in love with your indomitable courage and spirit, little one, but when it comes to issues concerning his wife, Shiva tends to be a little sensitive and yes, even a little boorish. He will not take kindly to those who dare to presume they have the right to interfere in his relationship with his wife. You must promise not to get in the way when they are fighting each other. Instead let them hash it out themselves. Believe me, Parvati will always be more than a match for Shiva!'

'What are you going to do next?' Nesha piped up distractedly, making Karti understand what those wizened sages who proffered gems of wisdom generously only to be roundly ignored felt like. 'I hope you won't insist on seeing Mother and leave me with no choice but to beat you up with my staff. Though I promise it is not my intention to hurt you.'

The anger flared up again without warning, rising from a primeval part of him that could scarce be contained. *How dare the brat assume that she could even be compared with the Destroyer's son?* Karti struggled to tamp his runaway feelings down. He shuddered at the thought of her provoking Shiva the same way. Little Nesha liked playing with fire, she did.

'I will wait till she has calmed down before attempting to see her again,' he said slowly, deciding that at least one person needed to behave with a modicum of sense to keep the volatile situation from spiralling out of all control. 'In the meantime, you can tell her from me that she is being unreasonable as well as reckless and ought not to drag you into this.'

'She is going to be so furious with you!' Nesha informed him with morbid satisfaction.

'Oh! She finds it impossible to stay angry with me,' he said airily, 'though she may take out her ire on the naughty little girl who forgot her guard duties when plied with generous helpings of sweetmeats and consorted readily enough with Shiva's son who ran away with her enemy's daughter.'

Nesha hit him with her staff but he dodged it with the lightning quick reflexes he was famed for. Laughing aloud at her outrage, Kartikeya decided he had been worrying unduly. Shiva would not be able to resist Parvati's daughter any more than he could.

Parvati was watching her children. After what felt like entire lifetimes, she felt happiness flood her being, leaving her with a tingling rush of well-being. Dearest Kartikeya! He always had that effect on her. She knew how possessive he was where she was concerned and yet unlike Shiva, he had risen above his jealousy.

Forgetting every one of her numerous grievances against him, Parvati was tempted to rush out and hug her children to pieces. She almost did it too. Almost.

Divine Dissent

KARTIKEYA SUPPOSED HE ought to pay his father a visit but he had had about all he could take of his family for a while. He missed Devasena but couldn't help but wonder if eventually their love wouldn't prove enough to stop them from hating or fighting fit to kill each other. The thought depressed him and he decided to take off by himself for a bit just to clear his head.

It was not a good feeling to be aware that a potentially incendiary situation was well on its way towards exploding and he was completely powerless to do anything about it. How was it that he who had found a way to deal with tyrants and madmen without breaking into a sweat found himself out of his depths in matters of the heart? The long walk did not have the intended effect and Karti felt his tension mount in slow spirals, gathering momentum with every twisting turn.

Later, he had no recollection of how far his feet had taken him or how long he had been away. All he remembered was the agonizing regret that he had not stayed behind or gone to his father. Perhaps he should have done more than give pithy advice to Nesha, especially since he had known that she would discard it. When his worst fears had materialized, there wasn't a single thing he could do.

Responding to his urgent need, Chitra materialized by his side and they had made haste to return to Parvati's abode. But it was too late. What made it a hundred times worse was that it felt like he was actually there as the tragedy unfolded. Shiva's fury buffeted against him with such force, he could barely breathe and mother's agony lacerated his own heart. Then there was Nesha…little warrior, with the bluff honesty and partiality for sweetmeats. All he wanted was to reach them in time to shield her with his own body.

Shiva was calling out over and over again like one demented to his wife, insisting that she let him in. 'I just want to talk to you! Why won't you see me? Do I have to get on my knees and beg for the right to speak to my wife?

Parvati! Parvati! PARVATI!! Let me in! Tell your accursed brat to get out of the way or you will be sorry!'

His wife was shaking with disdain and cold fury, locked away in her private apartments, refusing to budge an inch, painfully aware that she had gone too far but unwilling to retrace her footsteps. If Shiva wished to take out his wrath on her, he was welcome to try! A lot of good it would do him!

The Destroyer cut a fearsome figure, his matted locks lashing against his cheeks, his eyes liquid pools of burning anger as he drew himself up to his full height. The serpents writhed and twisted against his adamantine form, hissing in warning. Ganga screamed hysterically as her waters came to a boil, simmering on the molten heat of his passion. Mortal and immortal alike would have died of fright had he glowered at them like that, the very incarnation of doom. For the first time, Kartikeya himself experienced dread fear coursing through his being leaving him weak with terror.

Little Nesha barely batted an eyelid as her antagonist towered over, his every move signalling his deadly intentions which his daughter ignored with supreme nonchalance. 'No, Nesha!' Kartikeya screamed across the distance that separated them, and Chitra flew so fast even Garuda would have been hard pressed to outpace him, but it wasn't nearly enough.

'GET OUT OF HIS WAY!' *Kartikeya's voice boomed across space but Nesha wouldn't pay heed. Her own blinding rage was a staccato beat in her ears and she was determined that Shiva would not pass.* 'Go away, you beast! My mother, greatest of the Goddesses, deserves better than you! Leave now before I am forced to kill you in order to set her…'

The golden Parashu, Shiva's mighty axe, came down in a killing arc and Karti would have gladly given his life and soul to stop its inexorable descent. A red veil seemed to obscure his father's vision, black fury flooding through his senses, slamming everything else aside, as he hacked cleanly through the neck separating a little head with wondrous curls and flashing eyes so like his own from the sturdy body that still stood erect and proud.

Parvati arrived on the scene just as the head rolled to a stop at her feet. She gazed at it dumbstruck with horror, too stunned for tears. Shiva's expression mirrored her own. He fell to his knees, staring at the lifeless body, bewilderment writ large on his features as if he couldn't figure out for the life of him, how it was that the lifeless body of their daughter lay between them.

He did not dare look up but even so, the force of her hatred and sorrow caused him to stagger backward. When she spoke, her voice was a whiplash.

'My daughter is gone! I cannot forgive you for this and this time you will pay for your arrogance. The three worlds will be the funeral pyre on which she will be cremated and you will burn with the rest of them. Consider that an act of kindness, for were I to let you live, every aeon of your existence across eternity will be wracked with agony and unceasing torment, long after you repent for the crime you have committed on this day. No matter how fast and far you run, there will be no escaping my wrath.'

'Please don't, Mother!' Kartikeya came in. Seeing the sight in front of him and hearing her words, his heart felt like it must break in two. Quietly he placed an arm on his father's shoulders which were shaking with grief. Shiva was crouched beside Nesha's body like a wounded animal, sobbing like the child he sometimes was. Taking off his own upper garment, Kartikeya covered Nesha's remains gently. The small gesture set off the tears that Parvati had not even known she was holding back.

'Enough is enough,' Karti went on firmly. 'We have all suffered enough. The three worlds need not partake of our grief.'

'I cannot live without my child!' She said the words simply, but they bespoke the full might of her iron will that refused to be denied retribution.

'None of us can,' Karti agreed. 'But it was you who taught me by example that no good can ever come from anger and retribution. Releasing your Shaktis to destroy everything in creation will not bring Nesha back. But I know someone who can. He is the benevolent God I have always worshipped.'

Shiva looked up at him, calm resolution finally replacing

his wild despair. 'Strike off the head off the first creature that crosses your path and is willing to give up its life in order that my child may live. Bring it to me immediately!'

Karti was gone even before he had uttered the last word. Shiva picked up the body and held it cradled in his arms. Parvati wept softly. How like her husband to hold his child with so much affection but only after he had succeeded in killing her!

'She was so brave,' he said it with such fierce pride, that Parvati felt long dormant tenderness stir in her breast, rekindling old feelings that she had believed dead and gone. 'There was so much wisdom and calm understanding in those eyes. She seemed aware that death is what I have to give and unlike anybody before her, there was graceful acceptance of the fact that terrible though it is, death is nevertheless my gift to the three worlds. It was only then that I realized that I loved this precious child and always did. I would have given anything to stop myself from doing what I did.'

Parvati's legs gave out and Shiva steadied her with one arm, lowering her head onto his lap where Nesha lay as if in repose, her flesh still soft and warm to the touch. 'What happened to us?' Parvati asked him softly, knowing that he did not know either. 'I just want things to go back to the way they were when we were not fighting so bitterly. How could we have squandered away the great love we have for each other? Of everything that has happened, that is the most unpardonable and we can never allow it to happen again. Promise me that we will be happy and in love again.'

'I promise!' Shiva whispered, kissing her gently on the forehead. They looked up as Kartikeya entered, he was out of breath and in his right hand he held the head of an elephant with a single tusk. Not far from here, the former scourge of the three worlds had been waiting for him, ready and willing to do what he must, in order that an irreplaceably special being could be returned to the three worlds.

I will find a way to repay you for the kindness and favour you have shown me today. Kartikeya was so grateful, he was in tears. Tarakasura had been as good as his word and had repaid the debt a thousand times over. Kartikeya had blessed Maya's noble son with all his heart and departed, having relieved him of his elephant head.

Parvati rose quickly to her feet and went to his side. Shiva placed Nesha carefully on the floor and reached up to accept the head. He worked quickly to affix it onto the neck, his fingers a whirl of dexterity as he carried out the intricate procedure with skill and precision, putting painstaking effort into it and all the love that he could muster.

Kartikeya placed a comforting arm around Parvati's shoulders and she melted into his embrace. 'How could I have ever doubted you? I should have known that you would always be there when needed.'

Kartikeya kissed her on top of the head, too overcome to speak. Parvati looked up at him. 'You can tell my daughter-in-law that this is her home now and she will always be welcome to grace our abode with her presence.'

'Don't tell anybody but you are the great love of my life!' Karti whispered to her.

'And you are mine!' she whispered back.

Shiva stepped back and they watched in amazement as life manifested itself on the remains of death. Before their very eyes, the child twitched as the body re-shaped itself to suit the new head. Nearly twice the size that it had originally been, with a thickened neck and shoulders that were even broader than

Shiva's, a magnificent youth rose to his feet a little shakily but steadying himself in an instant.

There was a wrinkle in Parvati's brow when she beheld the son who stood in place of her daughter. Karti whispered in her ear, 'My father can't help himself, you know, but even you will admit that he has outdone himself!'

'This is Ganesha!' Shiva introduced him to his mother, looking very much like a little boy himself, as he sought her approval. Parvati smiled at him despite herself.

Ganesha examined his gently curving trunk with unabashed delight and took in his corpulent form with the massive pot belly with amazement. 'All the better to hold the sweetmeats in!' he winked at the three of them, his voice a low rumble that was music to their ears. His eyes alighted on his brother first and with a squeal of delight, he launched himself at him, knocking Kartikeya clean over, nearly crushing him under his bulk.

'Now, Ganesha is as much mine as he is yours,' Shiva told Parvati, seeing the glow of love in her eyes after what felt like forever. 'He always was!' she whispered.

Lumbering over to his father, he touched his feet reverentially. 'I knew that you would not have the heart to kill me and leave me for dead, Father. On the other hand, I would not have been quite as merciful. My brother was right after all, there is a reason they call you Mahadeva!'

Parvati could not restrain herself and she threw her arms around him, unable to encircle his girth completely. 'Don't ever die for me again,' she breathed into his large ears and he flapped them in acquiescence, flippantly saying, 'I feel bad for my brother though, he is no longer the good-looking one in this family.'

'Don't feel too bad,' Karti grinned at him. 'Mother still loves me best!'

The four of them sat huddled together for the longest time, wishing they could stretch out the moment for all of eternity and perhaps they did manage the feat, for their collective happiness held them together forever more, past time, distance and the tumult that was theirs to shoulder. Their world was finally at peace. As was everything and everybody else in it.

A Fresh Start

$\mathcal{I}$T WAS A halcyon period. Devasena joined them in Kailash and Kartikeya decided that his happiness was complete. She got along famously with Shiva who had seldom been more blissful or inclined towards largesse. He seemed to be enjoying fatherhood and lavished all his attention on the boys and they soaked it all up.

Even Parvati and Devasena got over their initial dislike for each other and decided that they could easily bond by discussing all the things that Kartikeya did that they considered annoying in the extreme. Chitra and Ganesha enjoyed contributing to these lengthy exchanges too. Karti supposed it was their way of masking the excessive love and loyalty they bore him in order to avert the evil eye.

Ganesha was pampered silly by all the inhabitants of Kailash and he was so good-natured about all of it that Karti found he resented the attention showered on his brother only mildly. Still, having a sibling wasn't the worst thing in the world, especially when he hero-worshipped you. Ganesha followed Kartikeya everywhere and it wasn't as annoying as he had expected it to be.

Nothing lasted forever but that was how it ought to be, Karti found himself philosophizing, as the four of them sat together on a fine day. There were momentous happenings underfoot and Kartikeya had called the family meeting. His nuptials with Devasena had only recently been concluded. He had wanted a simple ceremony but their legions of devotees wouldn't hear of it and the entire thing had been an elaborate affair with enough wine to drown the three worlds in and so much food that even Ganesha claimed he was stuffed and couldn't eat another bite for an age though he was already snacking on the *modaks* Parvati was plying him with.

The *saptarishis* had showed up en masse and so had the Devas, Asuras and humans, along with the birds and animals. The celebrations had gone on for days and everybody blessed the radiant couple, presenting them with commemorative carved idols that were a likeness of the two of them, delicate ivory figurines, rare and exquisite pieces of jewellery made of heavy gold and precious stones, fine weaponry and other invaluable gifts.

Seeing Indra's only surviving family member made the Devas moist-eyed and they sang praises of the Princess and her chosen Lord. Devasena was touched with their devotion and her tears glistened like pearls as they ran down her lovely face. Kartikeya took her hand in his and squeezed gently. At that moment, they both realized what needed to be done if the ghosts of the past were to be laid to rest forever. Later, on their wedding night as they lay spent and filled with well-being, they had talked about their plans for the future at length.

Now that their decisions had been made, Kartikeya had decided to talk to his parents and Ganesha about it. They were looking at him expectantly and he cleared his throat before beginning. 'As you know, the Devas have repeatedly asked that I occupy the throne left vacant by Indra.' He paused. Parvati was looking agitated whereas Shiva appeared mildly curious. Ganesha alone had a knowing look on his face and he winked conspiratorially at his brother.

Kartikeya took a deep breath. 'I have no interest in ruling nor an appetite for the power games it entails or a stomach for the tedium of administration. Devasena respects my wishes in the matter; however, she felt that having lost their King, the Devas are like orphaned children and need a leader to guide them into the future. I suggested that the mantle of leadership would rest lightly on her capable shoulders and as Indra's heir, she is best suited for the job.'

Expecting them to be slackjawed with shock, Karti was not prepared for the warm applause of approbation that greeted his words. Ganesha swallowed his *modaks* before replying to his pronouncement, 'She is the perfect replacement for Indra who, it must be confessed, was a warmonger who had become intoxicated with power. Devasena, on the other hand, will usher in a new era of peace.'

Shiva thumped his shoulder and said, 'I was afraid that I was going to have to disown you. Imagine a son of mine lording it over the three words outfitted in silks, jewellery and an unwieldy crown! Those things would have suited you ill.'

Parvati was less enthused though. 'How exactly is this… unconventional arrangement going to work out? If Devasena is to rule the three worlds, where does that leave you? Besides a crown and a throne will suit her no better than it does you.

In addition to that, the Devas are a spent force and in a bid to recapture their glory days, they may just cause untold damage! If the past is any indication…'

'Don't you worry about a thing, Mother! Devasena is far too clever to make the mistakes her father did. She said that for too long the Devas have been enslaved by the trappings of power and have grown weak having wallowed excessively in wealth and plenty. She feels it is time they left their palaces and treasuries behind in order to return to their roots and renew their allegiance to Bhoomi Devi. It is her wish that the Devas and Asuras put aside their differences and usher in a new age, by working in tandem for the betterment of the three worlds.

'She feels that it is the only way to make amends for the violent course they charted for mortal and immortal alike by constantly grappling for power. In her words, the stain of blood can never be washed out by more blood; only service and sacrifice can do the trick.'

'I'll admit that Devasena can turn a pretty phrase, but are the Devas and Asuras in agreement with her idealistic plans? Surely the former have grown too accustomed to eating off gold plates and carousing in lakes filled with intoxicants while the latter haven't forgotten Indra's many plots to deprive them of their share of the loot plundered at the expense of the mortals? What if they resist whoever seeks to separate them from their ill-gotten gains?' Parvati voiced her doubts, wondering if her sweet daughter-in-law was equal to the task of dealing with the vipers' nest that was her father's family.

'Didn't Soora sack Amaravati and raze it to the ground?' Shiva pointed out. 'They don't have a fine city and luxuriant palaces to return to as yet. From what I hear, even Kubera's treasury has been emptied. For the time being at least, they won't mind pretending that their poverty-stricken status is one they have chosen and not been forced into.'

'Besides they will think twice about "resisting" Devasena, especially since Mahasena is her husband!' Ganesha pitched in.

Kartikeya shrugged, remembering his first battle which she had helped him bring to such a satisfactory conclusion. His wife was a lot tougher than they gave her credit for. 'I don't intend to interfere. She is perfectly capable of dealing with the Devas and their half-brothers on her own. I merely suggested that she request Vishnu to join this endeavour in an advisory capacity and she is presently on her way to Vaikuntam with Chitra to discuss all this with him. It will take a while but I have no doubt she will handle her transition to power with ease and make her dreams for a better tomorrow a reality.'

He paused, going over their lengthy conversations in his mind.

'I do look forward to this opportunity but it pains me to think that you will not be by my side,' she had said.

'You know I will be there whenever you need me,' he had reassured her.

Devasena nodded, cheering up considerably. 'I will miss you though, and Chitra as well. You are perfectly capable of giving your heart to another but your mount will always love me best.'

'Chitra is most distraught at the thought of the imminent parting but he did say that being married without actually doing any of the things being married entails is the only way to have a good marriage.'

Kartikeya was smiling when Parvati who was not done yet with her questions cut into his thoughts. 'But you still haven't told me your plans? Is it going to be your life's mission to reform evildoers and take lovers in an endless chain for the ostensible purpose of renewing Bhoomi Devi's energy source?'

'I have been thinking of travelling a bit, perhaps all the way to the deep South. The restlessness had been building inside me for a while now and I yearn to journey into the unknown, meet new faces and have unusual experiences. That beautiful, mysterious land seems to be exercising a magnetic pull over me and I would like to go there and get better acquainted with the place and its people.' He was being deliberately vague. 'Who knows what the future holds for me? I am very excited to find out.' Someone else was summoning him to the South with her persistent devotion but he wished to keep that to himself for now.

Shiva and Parvati exchanged a secret look which neither of their children who were hardly children anymore missed. 'The South is the land from which your mother originally hailed, long before fate decreed that she take birth as Himavan's daughter. They have never forgiven me for taking her away from them and bringing her to the snowy heights of my own Kailash, though I promised them that what they had given up will someday be returned to them. From the moment you were born, they have loved you as their own and believed that you belong to them.'

'My people can be ridiculous at times, and there is no need for you to give in to their every ludicrous whim,' Parvati interrupted. 'Whatever will people say if you leave your parents and wife behind to gallivant into parts unknown? They will assume that you left in high dudgeon over some imagined conflict!'

'Mother is right! There will be vile rumours circulating suggesting that you got miffed because I ate your share of the *modaks* though we agreed to race across the three worlds for it or something! Or that we fought over a girl's affections and you left, unable to bear the damage to your ego on being rejected,' Ganesha suggested with a grin.

Karti rolled his eyes. 'Who cares about gossipmongers and their unhealthy obsession with our family? You are so creative with the stories you should be a scribe, Ganesha! If you want to dissuade wagging tongues, why don't you get off your expanding backside and come along with me? We will spend our days adventuring and exploring!'

Ganesha rubbed his belly expansively. 'Do I look like someone who wishes to give up the comforts of his mother's home to root about in the wilderness and put up with a whole lot of inconveniences? I should think not. It is my plan to remain here and who knows, I may just become the scribe you suggested I become. However, since you asked, I will pay you the occasional visit to see how you are coping.'

Parvati was not at all happy about the way this conversation was going and was about to protest again when Shiva's voice sounded in her ear, 'Let him go to the land of the Tamils if that is what he wants. Kartikeya's destiny awaits him there, as you very well know.'

She was silent for a long while, before speaking in subdued accents. 'I couldn't be prouder of you, my son! Devasena is lucky to have a husband who is the wind at her back enabling her to soar across the three worlds in order to be the best she is capable of being. In future, if mothers were to raise their sons in your image, the mortals and immortals will be spared much strife and suffering.'

'Of course, Kartikeya is your son now,' Shiva grumbled. 'Tomorrow if he were to meet a beautiful girl from the South and offer her his heart, he will no doubt become my son again.'

Parvati thought it wasn't the best of jokes, but you wouldn't know it from the way the three of them doubled over laughing. She would have been annoyed if it weren't for her excessive fondness for the rambunctious trio.

Love Again

GANESHA WAS AS good as his word. He took his time but he did manage to follow his brother to a little hill in the Southern region, the name of which he had difficulty pronouncing, because in order to say 'Pazhani' right, you needed to roll your tongue just so, and he had difficulty getting the hang of it. Kartikeya was delighted to see him, as was Chitra.

'The natives have taken you to their hearts and seem unwilling to let go,' Ganesha began. 'Already there are more shrines than I could count built in your honour as well as exquisite poetry, music and songs composed in your name. They told me stirring tales of your many deeds of valour and referred to you as their saviour and protector. Mother and Father are going to be so proud. It must be nice to be so universally adored.'

'Oh, stop it!' Karti shoved him playfully. 'I heard that you are much *more* revered and that people have bestowed the somewhat pompous honorific "Smasher of Obstacles" upon you and seek your blessings before setting out on new ventures. Your talent as a scribe has also come in for a lot of appreciation, though I remember getting annoyed when you refused to play outside with me, preferring to sit at Mother's side transcribing her thoughts on my heroism for posterity. But in all seriousness, I could not be prouder of you.'

'Now that we have established that this family takes a lot of pride in each other's achievements when we are not bent on killing each other, shall we move on? How are things with Devasena?'

Kartikeya beamed in response, and said, 'We don't meet as often as either of us would like but she has done exemplary work in so short a while. The Devas as well as Asuras have accepted her as their leader and with Vishnu to guide them, they have wrought miracles. Their chosen path requires steady plodding and unfortunately no songs will be written about their efforts but Devasena does not seem to mind. She says that hard work and service are its own rewards and must be undertaken without expectation of fame, praise or glory.'

'My sister-in-law is truly special,' Ganesh said with open admiration. 'But speaking of Vishnu, I am actually here at his behest.'

'What does he want from me?', Kartikeya asked him.

'Vishnu seems to be in a bit of a quandary. It is a long story but a charming one. The sage Kanva cursed him and the Goddess Lakshmi for failing to fall over themselves in their eagerness to greet him when he honoured them with a visit. Consequently, the divine duo took birth on Mother Earth, the former as the dumb saint Sivamuni and the latter as a deer. Unable to bear the separation, the sage and deer sought each other out for a brief tryst. From their union, a beautiful child was born. But the deer, seeing that its form was human and having no notion of the significance of this birth, abandoned the baby and returned to the wild.

'This is the part that concerns you. This child, called Valli, was raised by the tribal chieftain Nambi, and is destined to be yours. Having grown up hearing tales of your valour, she swore that she would marry none but you and spends her days in silent devotion waiting to be united with her one true love. When that happens, Sivamuni and the deer will be free to return to the divine form from which they emerged.'

Chitra was pleased that Ganesha had finally come to the end of his long-winded speech. 'Thank you very much for the information but as Garuda's son, I am familiar with this tale and Kartikeya here is smitten with the lovely Valli and has already made her acquaintance. I am sorry you made his long journey just to tell us the things we already knew.'

'I have always wondered what you would taste like when cooked over a slow flame,' Ganesha said, looking at Chitra with a hungry gleam in his eyes. 'And for your information, I have been told that I am the best storyteller there ever was and that my voice has a mellifluous, hypnotic quality that makes my audience want to listen for all of eternity.'

'Actually, I have wondered the same thing quite often! I am sure he will taste delicious. And even Chitra will admit that Ganesha is the better storyteller!' Kartikeya chimed in and the two of them burst into raucous laughter as Chitra stalked away.

Kartikeya smiled, 'I have known about Valli since the time I came into being. Devasena, Valli and I are united by a bond that goes back a long way. In fact, it was for her that I made the journey to these parts. She is fire made flesh and the cold North is no place for her.'

There was a tenderness in his eyes Ganesha had never seen before. It amused him and made him feel a tad protective about his brother. If Kartikeya had a flaw, it was his deep and abiding passion for all things. But it was also his strength. Ganesha, unlike him, had been made in the image of his mother before being remade by his father. Inadvertently, it was in him that they had achieved the balance between the equal but opposing forces of *purusha* and *prakriti*. His second lease of life had given him an equanimity that could never be perturbed. Unlike Kartikeya, he would know neither pain nor pleasure. It was *his* greatest strength and weakness.

While Ganesha was lost in his pontificating, Kartikeya's thoughts turned to Valli, the way they had been doing for a while now. Nambi and his sons were extremely protective of this jewel among women and made sure that she was never alone. Yet, he alone knew that she was always alone. Lonely in the middle of the loved ones who were with her at all times. Alone with her thoughts. Of him.

Aching to draw closer to her, Kartikeya decided to exercise the creative powers Ganesha was famed for. He had gone to her in a variety of disguises. Sometimes he was a parrot that she carried on her shoulders all day and fed morsels to with her own hands. She was partial to the little rabbit too, petting and stroking its velvety fur while he grew comfortable on her lap. In recent times, he had taken to visiting her as a blind old man who carved the most exquisite ornaments and statuettes from ivory. They had become fast friends and she had taken to confiding in him.

'Is it true you will marry none but Shiva's son?' he had queried and when she replied in the affirmative, he pressed on, 'Perhaps you should reconsider your decision, little one... They say he is fierce, warlike and wishes to fill entire oceans with the blood of his enemies. When he is not killing, his preferred pastime is the seduction of ladies. His followers are worse than him. These abominable creatures were women once but he has transformed them into monstrous fiends who attack babies in the womb, afflict children with illness and hound expecting mothers to their death. Why would you give your heart to someone like that?'

Valli smiled a secret smile, thinking he would not notice, and replied, 'They also say that he is noble and handsome, and that his strength lies in the compassion he shows those who are weaker than him. That he is the protector of women, children and just about everybody who needs help. But even if every word you uttered were proved true, I would still love him unstintingly and without reservation. His wickedness would be every bit as appealing as his virtue simply because both are a part of him.'

The blind old man shook his head despairingly, though his heart was singing. 'I cannot stop you from the pursuit of such folly, but I am a little curious. What if this Kartikeya does not reciprocate your love? Besides, he is already married to Indra's daughter Devasena and defied his mother to be with her. If he were to leave her for you, wouldn't that make him unfaithful and a cheat?'

'Not necessarily,' she told him patiently. 'The practice of polygamy and polyandry are not unprecedented, especially if it's by mutual choice. All I know is that loving someone does not mean chaining them and never letting go. On the contrary, it means setting your love free. Besides, you did tell me once that Parvati wasn't too fond of Devasena initially, but from what I hear, they have learned to bury the hatchet and let bygones be bygones. In the extremely likely event that Devasena and I don't take to each other, we too can try and keep things polite or even cordial for our husband's sake.

'Besides, I doubt Devasena will have much time for either of us, married as she is to her duty and the thankless task of coaxing the Devas and Asuras to actually do some good when they would rather focus on their petty differences, blow it out of all proportion and kill each other. Still, it is a worthy effort and she has my respect, if not my love.'

'I am only a blind man and clearly no match for your dazzling wit and infallible rationale. If you choose to marry Kartikeya and voluntarily enter into an extremely volatile situation that may blow up in your face at any moment, then I cannot stop you. Having spent your life dreaming of perfection, I can only hope reality will not prove too disappointing!'

No sooner had Kartikeya said the words than he wished he could take it back. It had not been his intention to ruin her dreams of the future with a forced helping of harsh truth. To his relief, though, she seemed unperturbed, as she said sweetly, 'My reality will always be what I make of it. There is no need for you to worry!'

He smiled at her. 'Kartikeya is lucky indeed to have you in his life. He must have done something right in addition to all his killing and lovemaking to have earned you as his reward. You will, no doubt have beautiful babies; I have heard tell that he is quite good-looking.' The old man scratched an evil-looking wart on his nose. 'Girls always forgive these classically handsome devils all their shortcomings, but they are harsher on the likes of me. Why should you be an exception?'

'Pray tell me, when have I ever been harsh to you? We have known each other only for a short time but already I think of you as a dear friend. Ultimately the people who matter do so because of the way they make you feel.'

'You have an answer for everything, pretty maiden, but as my mother says, words are wind and the harsh truth is that no girl is going to insist on marrying me. But I am too old for love anyway. You still haven't said what you will do if he does not reciprocate your love?' There was a sly note in his voice which she ignored.

'There isn't the remotest chance of that happening,' she said with absolute certainty. 'He will love me as much as I love him. In fact, for a while now I have realized that he is closer to me than ever before. Thanks to his proximity, I derive the utmost joy from the most mundane things like a naughty parrot nibbling on my earlobe or a rabbit snuggling in my lap. Even a cynical old man such as yourself who doubts the power of my love makes me deliriously happy. He is near, you will see and when he reveals himself to me...'

'You don't have to tell me. When Kartikeya deigns to accept your love, the two of you will break into song and dance as if that were a normal or natural thing to do and sicken everybody in the vicinity with cloying displays of affection.' He spat out a gob of saliva in case he hadn't made his disdain clear.

Valli's laughter rang out, 'You don't know me as well as you think you do. When Kartikeya comes to me, I will slap him really hard across the face.' His shock made her laugh some more. 'It will serve him right for taking his own sweet time to come to me.'

'Kartikeya! Kartikeya! You have disappeared into your dreams and it is better if you return to reality if you want to make them come true!' Ganesha was shaking him by the shoulders. 'It is time for you to declare your love for the redoubtable Valli, before you lose whatever is left of that fine head. By the way, Mother and Devasena are going to be so happy when they find out about your newest and greatest love!'

'Father will bear the brunt of it, as per usual,' Kartikeya chuckled. 'Isn't it funny that no matter how much things change...'

'...they still remain the same. Let us refrain from using overblown clichés and resolve this matter of the heart as quickly as possible. All this nonsense about an overprotective father and brothers is all eyewash. As if any of them could ever be a match for Shiva and Parvati's sons! You just want to prolong the romance endlessly!'

Impulsively, Kartikeya hugged his brother. Together they set off in search of Valli. They found her in the fields where her job was to scare away the birds that were helping themselves to the grain. She was feeding them nuts and berries in a bid to dissuade them from wrecking her father's property.

Without warning, an elephant tore through the fields, moving with surprising speed for a creature of its bulk. Deaf to the shouts of alarm, Valli could only watch in mute horror as it came directly towards her. The beast was so close, it would only be a matter of moments before he skewered her with a single tusk.

It was the moment when Valli was confronted by the face of death, drawing ever closer, keen to snatch her away when happiness was close to her grasp. How could it be? She straightened herself up, a smile suddenly brightening her features. Even the charging elephant looked surprised confirming her suspicion.

'Run, Valli!' As one, the voices beseeched her to take herself out of harm's way. And still, she stood rooted to the spot, a strange look of joy on her face.

'Lord Kartikeya! Save your beloved! Don't let her die! Kill the fiendish beast!'

Valli tuned out the voices. Her Lord was close and he would be with her soon. She was so impatient it hurt. Hadn't she said as much to her dear friend so very recently?

Suddenly, the blind old man was by her side. 'Take my hand!' he said, holding out a frail, spotted hand that was shaking with age. 'I am your only hope.'

Valli refused to take his hand but she was as good as her word and her palm struck his face in a stinging blow. Ganesha came to a screeching halt, stunned by the unexpected turn of events. Karti was doubled over with laughter, though. When he rose to his full height and stood before her in his true form, Valli was overcome with shyness and she buried his face in her chest. Everything else disappeared into the haze. The elephant, fields, family and friends. He was all she had ever wanted and in his loving embrace, she lacked for nothing. Forever more, this would be her reality.

Kartikeya felt her complete happiness because it was his too. There would be time for the others later. But for now it was just him and her. It was more than enough.

Ganesha left them that way. This was like the happy endings he wrote about in his stories, though he wasn't much of a believer in them when it came right down to it. Still, even if this wasn't quite the same thing, it had to be the next best thing. Which was even better.